The
Black
Stallion's
Shadow

→STEVEN FARLEY←

Random House 🏠 New York

For valuable advice and support, I'd like to thank my editor, Jenny Fanelli, and two of the film world's most renowned horse trainers, Glen Randall Sr. and Corky Randall.

Library of Congress Cataloging-in-Publication Data: Farley, Steven. The black stallion's shadow / by Steven Farley. p. cm. — (The Black stallion series) SUMMARY: The Black suddenly develops a fear of shadows that threatens his career as a racehorse. 1. Horses—Juvenile fiction. [1. Horses—Fiction.] I. Title. II. Series: Farley, Walter. Black stallion series. PZ10.3.F22Bmh 1995 [Fic] 94-41239 ISBN: 0-679-85004-X (trade hardcover)

Manufactured in the United States of America 10 9 8 7 6 5 4 3 2 1

To Val and Or

Contents

Contents

The
Black
Stallion's
Shadow

→ CHAPTER 1 ←

Riders Up!

I t was American Cup day at Santa Anna, the highlight
of the winter racing season. Less than forty-five minutes remained before the race. Down in the
windowless jockeys' room, Alec Ramsay stood in front of
his open locker. He took a deep breath to calm his nerves.
The air tasted of saddle soap and sweat.

Alec always felt a little uneasy before a big race, but
today his stomach was doing flip-flops. He hoped the
worry didn't show. A mirror hung on the inside of the
locker door. In the glass Alec could see his tanned face,
high forehead and close-cropped red hair. Clear plastic
riding goggles hung loosely from his neck. His expression
gave away nothing despite the hollowness he felt inside.

Aside from the banks of lockers lining the walls, the
jockeys' room looked and sounded like a subterranean
recreation center. TV monitors hung from the ceiling.

Game and card tables, installed to help the jockeys relax between races, were crowded. Small groups of tough, wiry men lounged about playing cards or Ping-Pong to pass the time. Like Alec, most wore long terry-cloth bathrobes. They bantered in Spanish and English.

A replay of the sixth race flashed by on the closed-circuit TV monitors. Alec looked over to the nearest screen. His eyes followed the horses crossing the finish line, but his thoughts remained far away.

The local papers were predicting an upset for his horse, the Black, in the American Cup race. Ordinarily Alec would think of such talk as a promotional gimmick to draw more fans to the track. But this time the sports gossip bothered him more than usual.

No horse could keep winning races forever, Alec knew, not even the Black. The fact haunted him. Could he push his horse until the day some young giant-killer dealt the stallion a humiliating defeat? The current West Coast champion, an unbeaten colt named Ruskin, just might be the one to do it. Taking on Ruskin would have been tough even at Belmont or Aqueduct, Alec's local New York tracks. Here on Ruskin's home turf it could prove devastating.

To make matters worse, Alec needed this race—and the $250,000 purse—badly. A win would pump up the prices for Hopeful Farm's stock at the yearling sale next week back in New York. The Black was, in effect, representing all the other horses on the farm. If Alec's family couldn't get top dollar for their horses, it meant trouble for the financially strapped farm. Alec swallowed. His body felt tense and his throat was dry. Too much was at stake for this to be just another race.

Picking up the light racing saddle and pads, Alec walked over to the scales to weigh out. The frail, white-faced clerk of the scales watched the needle swing to 110 pounds and steady. The clerk marked a piece of paper attached to his clipboard. "Okay, Ramsay, that'll do," he said, and motioned Alec to get down. "Next."

Some of the other riders in the seventh race were already making their way along the basement hallway. Alec passed the security guard posted at the door and followed after them. They climbed a worn staircase leading to ground level.

As the jockeys filed into the paddock Alec caught sight of the Black. Never before was there such a magnificent horse, Alec thought. The Black was one of a kind.

The Black's trainer, Henry Dailey, walked the stallion back and forth in front of the dozen partitioned saddling stalls that ran the length of the paddock. Alec watched his horse move as if seeing him for the first time. The stallion held his small Arabian head high atop a long graceful neck joining a thoroughbred's body. Sunlight glistened on the jet black of his coat. At seventeen hands the Black was a giant of a horse, a study in beauty and well-balanced muscles. Every part fit together perfectly. Henry put it simply: "The Black has what a horse is supposed to have and has it where a horse is supposed to have it."

The old trainer spotted Alec, and his impish blue eyes lit up. Alec smiled back. Aside from the difference in their ages, Alec and Henry were much alike. Between them was a bond as strong as blood—the love of horses, and of one horse in particular, the Black.

Alec looked up at the tote board recording the wagering for the upcoming race. Despite the Black's experience and near-flawless record, the odds makers favored Ruskin to win the American Cup today. Who could blame them? Earlier that season the colt had shattered track records at nearby Hollywood Park and Del Mar Racetrack outside of San Diego. One sportswriter said that Ruskin must have an Indy 500 car in his bloodlines.

Ruskin was what every established champion feared most: a hard-charging up-and-comer hungry for victory. Alec saw him waiting patiently in his open-ended saddling stall. Ruskin's copper-colored coat set off the curves and bulges of deep shoulders and a broad back. The coat seemed drawn too tight, as if he were outgrowing it. Thick layers of muscle filled out his tremendous neck and quarters. Ruskin's jockey would be Hector Morales, a Santa Anna regular with a fine record of his own. Alec knew this was going to be a tight race, and he was getting more nervous by the second.

"Take ahold there, Alec," Henry said as he handed Alec the reins. Henry bent down to tighten the saddle's girth strap. The Black raised a hind leg and stomped the ground. "Whoa," Henry said firmly. The Black's eyes were bright and alert. He dipped his head and restlessly chewed at the bit in his mouth. Alec faced his horse and gently rubbed the Black's forehead.

In and around the other saddling stalls owners and trainers smiled and talked together. Carrioca, the only filly in the field, was owned by Billy Mars, a famous rock-and-roll star. With his shoulder-length black hair and flashy white suit, Mars was attracting as much attention as his horse.

"Riders up," called the patrol judge. Henry gave Alec a boost, and the young jockey eased himself into his saddle. Morales was already atop Ruskin. The colt stepped out onto the walking ring to circle the paddock one last time before heading out to the track. Alec and Henry watched Morales ride by on the statuesque two-year-old. Ruskin moved gracefully and with deliberate strides, lifting and placing his hooves with perfect precision.

Morales carried a whip tucked under his arm. "Take a good look, Ramsay," he teased Alec. "'Cause all you gonna see in this race is my colt's tail flappin' in you face."

Henry scowled. "Wise guy," the old-timer grunted. Alec pretended to laugh off the cocky comment. Morales had a reputation for being a joker. But whatever else people said about him, no one could deny that he was all pro, as was Ruskin's trainer, Luke Larsen. Only one thing mattered to Larsen. Winning. For the Cup race, Larsen had coupled Ruskin's entry with another colt, the sprinter Cielo Grande. To the bettors this was like getting two horses for the price of one.

Both Henry and Alec noted the coupling of Cielo and Ruskin and guessed that Larsen planned to use Cielo as a pacesetter, a "rabbit." When the front runners grew tired from chasing Cielo, Ruskin could make a come-from-behind charge down the homestretch. The strategy was as old as racing itself and perfectly legal. The apprentice jockey Tommy Canter had been chosen to ride the lanky gray Cielo. As an apprentice, Canter was entitled to carry less weight than the veteran riders, a valuable asset when riding a rabbit.

Alec turned to Henry for any final instructions. Not that he needed them; it was more of a ceremonial gesture at this point in their careers. But today Henry knew something was bothering his jockey.

"What's the matter, kid? You okay?" Henry whispered out of the side of his mouth.

"I guess so," Alec replied uneasily.

"You guess?"

"I'm okay," Alec said.

"Listen, Alec. Forget those stories in the paper. Everything'll be fine, you'll see. Just ride the race the way she comes up. You know what to do."

Despite Henry's confident words Alec could see the furrows deepen in the old trainer's wrinkled brow. So the stories in the paper had gotten to him too. Henry looked as though he knew very well what was at risk here today.

Cameras clicked as horses, jockeys and outriders filed onto the track for the post parade. By sheer size alone the Black and Ruskin stood out from the rest. The spectators oohed and aahed at the sight of the horses.

The Black warmed up nicely in front of the grandstand, and some of Alec's confidence began to return. The stallion was ready to race. Alec tested the spring in his stirrups, crouching forward above the Black's neck. The Black eagerly responded to the shifting weight on his back until Alec pulled him up again.

Earlier in the day the smog had lifted to reveal in the distance the rugged San Gabriel Mountains outside Los Angeles. They were a stunning backdrop, and Santa Anna was widely regarded as one of the most beautiful tracks in the country. Thousands of noisy spectators jammed the towering grandstands. At the end of the homestretch stood the ornately decorated clubhouse, surrounded by landscaped gardens and also packed with racing fans.

As the warm afternoon sun moved behind the stands, it cast a long shadow down across the track and into the infield, where still more spectators thronged. Radios blared rock music in homage to Billy Mars and his filly. Beyond the spreading shadow some of the fans had stripped down to their bare backs to enjoy the warm sunshine. Here and there low-hanging clouds dotted the sky.

The starting gate, a jangling network of slats, bars and doors, was pulled by a tractor to the beginning of the homestretch. Alec looked up and down the straightaway. The first part of the mile-and-a-half course would be a flat-out sprint down the homestretch in front of the stands. Then they would ride all the way around the racecourse and pass the stands a second time for the finish. To loosen up, Alec rode the Black beyond the start to the backstretch before returning to the gate.

Alec eased the Black to the outside of the track and waited. Soon the metallic voice of the track announcer drifted his way on the breeze. "Ladies and gentlemen, the horses are now entering the starting gate. One minute until post time."

The horses who had drawn the inside starting positions were loaded first. One by one the assistant starters led the nine horses to their stalls. Quickly the doors clanged shut behind them. In a moment the Black's stall was before him and a starter waved him in. The stallion loaded easily into post position seven.

Alec pulled his riding goggles over his eyes and found a spot to focus on at the far end of the straightaway. Carrioca banged impatiently against the walls of her padded stall. "Settle that filly down, Gill," the starter ordered the filly's jockey. The assistants climbed in and out of the gate like monkeys, trying to keep the horses still.

Automatically Alec steadied the Black before he too began fidgeting. He rubbed the Black's neck and whispered to his horse, "Wait for me."

The last stall door clicked shut. The outside horse was finally in place. Alec grabbed a fistful of mane. It would help him keep his balance in the early going. He pulled himself forward and braced for the break onto the track.

A cloud passed over the sun and the shadows on the track disappeared. A brief moment of calm settled on the waiting horses. The starter hit the switch and the gates flew open. The American Cup was on!

✧ CHAPTER 2 ✦

The
American Cup

The horses broke from the gate like a cavalry charge. Driving hooves scrambled for traction and tore up the racetrack. Hoofbeats exploded like gunfire. "Ya, ya, ya!" shouted the jockeys. Their horses surged ahead, blowing deep lungfuls of air through distended nostrils. Alec bounced to a crouch. The Black took two strides, dropped his head and stumbled! Dirt splattered onto Alec's goggles. He sat tight and gave his horse time to collect himself.

The Black fell to last place before finding solid footing and digging in. Alec moved his arms low to his horse's neck and tucked himself into the streaming mane. His legs became shock absorbers locked into the stirrups. Hunching over, he felt the familiar surge beneath him like a surfer being picked up by a powerful ocean swell.

As expected, the early lead belonged to Cielo, the "rabbit." The apprentice jockey Tommy Canter was struggling to keep his balance astride the front runner. Morales eased off on Ruskin and dropped back to fourth place.

Fractions flashed by on the tote board's electronic teletimer. Alec counted the time in his head. He didn't need to look at a clock to know how fast they were going. The pace was much too quick for a race this long. Any horses trying to keep up with Cielo would be exhausted by the time they reached the homestretch.

The crowd of spectators had been on its feet since before the start of the race. The tumultuous roar from the stands, the wall of noise, sounded like a great wave about to crash down on the track. The Black moved up into the center of the horses as they crowded into the clubhouse turn. He wanted to keep going, but Alec checked him. The stallion shook his head, angered at being restrained.

"Easy, Black, easy. Plenty of time," Alec coaxed. He was rating his horse, saving the stallion's best effort for last. The trick would be knowing when and where to move.

Down the backstretch the furious pace began to take its toll. The gap narrowed between Cielo and the rest of the field. Alec slowly began to thread his way through the pack. Above the Black's pitched ears he saw Ruskin, cruising along smooth and steady. He was a length ahead, in third-place position.

Alec inched alongside Morales. The sculpted heads of Ruskin and the Black rose and dipped together as the horses rounded the far turn. On Alec's cue the Black switched to a left lead and went for the bit. Alec let him have it. The message was telegraphed and received. Go!

Alec and the Black blended together into one animal. In stride they became an unstoppable racing machine. Almost too easily the Black pulled past Ruskin and bore down on the tiring front runners, Major Martin and Cielo. The rushing wind fanned the bonfire burning in his heart. His hooves hammered the dirt. With one more surge of power the stallion moved past the others and into the lead unchallenged.

Swift and easy came the Black's strides. It was a perfect melding together of strength and unwasted motion. Alec adjusted his weight subtly. His black boots pressed tightly against the stallion's upper back. He rocked in his seat to match the pumping motion of the Black's shoulders and neck. The stallion's mane whipped across his face as they dashed down the homestretch.

Suddenly the sound of rushing hooves exploded from behind. Alec didn't have to guess who the challenger would be. "Rus-kin! Rus-kin! Rus-kin!" came the chant from the stands.

"Go get him, Hector!" Tommy Canter yelled to Morales.

Ruskin closed in on the Black and pulled along the inside. The colt's hooves skipped over the dirt and seemed to barely touch the track before taking off again. He was practically flying.

Morales went for the whip, smacking his horse repeatedly on the belly and then showing it to him to urge him on. Alec set his jaw, and the skin drew tight about his cheekbones. His body pressure sent new signals to the Black, asking for more speed.

Ruskin and the Black ran alongside each other like a wagon team in the same invisible harness. Alec moved the Black closer to Ruskin, forcing Morales to switch the whip to his left hand. Ruskin responded by swinging to the outside and bumping into the Black. Instead of faltering from the jolt the Black only changed leads and raced even faster. Both horses reached out to strain for every inch of precious ground. They blew past the last furlong pole left before the wire. Only 220 yards more to go!

All eyes in the packed stands followed the two horses as they began their neck-and-neck drive to the wire. From private box seats to the grandstands, people waved and cheered wildly. The clamor rocked Santa Anna like an earthquake.

High overhead a patch of clouds drifted away from the sun. A curtain of shadow fell from the stands and spread out onto the track. The horses drew near the looming darkness. As the light shifted around them Alec glimpsed something incredible out of the corner of his eye. Ruskin broke rhythm and leapt into the air! The colt lost his balance coming down and tumbled to the ground. Morales catapulted out of his saddle.

All at once the wild cheering from the stands ceased. A great whooshing sound rose up in its place—the sound of tens of thousands of people gasping in horror.

The wire passed overhead. Alec heard cries and an awful thudding behind him. He didn't need to turn around to guess what had happened. A horse and rider were down, maybe more. Riding instinctively, Alec could think only of the Black. "You did it, fella," he whispered to him. "You did it." Alec shifted his weight back in the stir-rups.

The black stallion shortened his strides, his breath thundering. He continued all the way around the club-house turn before finally slowing to a walk.

Alec closed his eyes. How he would like to forget this race or just keep on going, ride away and not look back! In the depths of his mind a storm was brewing. But he would not, could not, let the storm overtake him. Not now. Don't think, just do, he told himself.

Instead of going directly to the winner's circle, Alec rode past the clubhouse. He came to the shaded area in front of the grandstand. Crumpled shapes lay in the dirt just short of the finish line—one horse, two jockeys. The horse was Ruskin. The colt was struggling to get up, his foreleg severely broken. Assistants tried to hold the injured horse still and finally managed to get him down again. Another horse, Spin Doctor, stood on three legs by the inside rail.

A sick feeling knotted Alec's stomach. A flood of emo-tion welled up inside him, the blossoming of a fear that he hid from his family, from Henry, even from himself. The fear boiled down to one simple truth. Every time he raced the Black, he risked losing the stallion forever.

Two ambulances plowed through the torn-up track, stopping in front of the grandstand. Paramedics jumped out to lift the jockeys onto stretchers. Two special horse vans, the equine ambulances, drove out onto the track.

The veterinarians and their assistants gathered around the horses. They loaded Spin Doctor into one of the vans and drove away.

The other horse van pulled up beside Ruskin. While the assistants held the fallen horse still, a small group of men huddled together. Alec recognized one of them as Ruskin's trainer, Luke Larsen. A moment later a wide screen was propped up between Ruskin and the grandstand, shielding the red colt from view. Those who lived around the horse-racing game knew what this meant. When the screen went up, it signaled only one thing: a humane but certain death.

CHAPTER 3

Replay

At the sight of the screen, more cries of anguish and disbelief rose up from the crowd in the stands. Some people began weeping openly. Even hardened track regulars turned away and lowered their heads.

No matter how many times Alec had seen a horse put down, there was no getting used to it. Yet he understood very well that a horse with a broken leg was almost always doomed. The physiology of horses was very different from that of humans. Unable to stand while healing, the injured horse's organs would become misplaced during recovery. Giving Ruskin a fatal injection saved him the agony of a lingering death.

Alec rode back to the clubhouse and the gap in the fence that led to the winner's circle. Henry met him halfway there. The old trainer thrust a gnarled hand up to the Black's bridle and clipped on the lead shank. News photographers pushed their way through the crowd. They jumped out onto the track to snap photos of the victorious Black. The Black reared slightly. He fanned his nostrils and snorted. Henry jostled the photographers out of the way.

Police opened up a path through the crowd and into the enclosure. At a nod from the official Alec jumped off, unbuckled the girth strap and took his saddle to weigh out.

Word came in over the PA system that Spin Doctor's jockey, Victor Velazquez, had survived his fall bruised but unhurt. Ruskin's Hector Morales had been taken to the hospital. Spin Doctor's condition remained in question. Ruskin, the undefeated champion of California racing, was dead.

The track officials briefly went through the motions of the presentation ceremony. The usual smiles and con-gratulations were absent. No one really seemed to care about the order of finish. It had to be the most solemn winner's circle anyone had ever seen. Today there could be no winners.

Alec politely accepted a silver trophy, the American Cup award. Though he felt uncomfortable, his face dis-played little emotion. It was the mask of a hardened pro. Henry took the $250,000 check on behalf of Hopeful Farm.

As they left the winner's circle, a burly man in a dark suit pushed his way through the crowd and caught Henry by the elbow. The man showed Henry a badge, identifying him as a United States marshal. He reminded the trainer that Hopeful Farm owed the federal government $226,372.59 in back taxes.

Henry barely flinched as the marshal served him with an attachment on the Black's winnings, taking nearly the entire purse. As *Blood Horse* magazine later reported it, Henry just smiled and said, "That's racing for you. Easy come, easy go."

Alec headed to the lockers to shower and put on some clean clothes. A pack of reporters chased after him, shouting questions. "Hey, Ramsay. Any contact between the Black and Ruskin?" "Didn't Ruskin have a nose in front before he went down?" "Any comment at all?" "Come on, Ramsay. Give us a break."

The young jockey held up a hand and waved them off. "Sorry, guys. No comment."

Henry led the Black back to the barn, where the stallion underwent the routine postrace urine and saliva tests. When Alec returned to the stable area, the reporters were gone. Henry had already washed the Black. Steam rose from the stallion's glistening coat. Standing there, he looked like the essence of strength and vitality, anything but delicate. But a tragedy like today's was a reminder of how incredibly fragile a racehorse really was, Alec thought.

He reached up to rub the Black's forehead. The stallion cocked his ears as Alec spoke to him. The words made little sense. Only the sounds and rhythms were important. The Black whinnied in reply. Muscles quivered beneath his beautifully smooth skin.

Henry covered the Black with a light cooler and clipped a lead shank onto his bridle.

"You look shell-shocked, Alec," Henry said.

"I wonder why," Alec snapped back.

"What's eating you, kid? We'll survive. At least there's enough prize money left over to cover our feed and travel expenses. And the Black ran like a champ today. You can't blame yourself for what happened to the colt."

"Am I allowed to have feelings, Henry? Is that okay?"

"Settle down now," Henry said. "I don't know who could have seen what happened out there and not been affected. But you and I both know the racetrack is no place for sentimentality."

Even if Henry was right, it still didn't change the way Alec felt. Without saying anything, he led the Black to the walking path. The old trainer shrugged. He found a seat on a tack trunk and began thumbing through a *Racing Form*.

Alec took his time walking and grooming the Black. Then Henry carefully inspected the stallion's legs and feet one more time. The Black seemed sound enough, the trainer concluded. He wasn't so sure about Alec.

Henry said he had some errands to do, so Alec went back to the motel alone. The Railbird Motel, where he and Henry had been staying for the past week, was situated right next to Santa Anna. Its proximity to the track made it a favorite with visiting horsemen. Alec stretched out on his bed and dozed restlessly.

The evening news declared that day to be "the darkest racing day of the year." The reporter replayed a videotape of the Cup race. For the first time Alec saw what had actually happened.

The tape ran in slow motion and picked up the race at the neck-and-neck charge down the homestretch. As Ruskin reached the shadow of the grandstand he tried to jump the outer edge. He must have mistaken the sharp contrast between light and dark for something at his feet. The jump was a fatal misstep. Extended to the maximum, he couldn't gather his legs beneath him again. He went off stride, crashing to the ground less than fifty yards from the finish. Again Alec heard the horrible gasping sound from the crowd in the stands. It was a sound he would never forget.

Spin Doctor, running a few lengths behind the leaders, tripped over the fallen Ruskin and his jockey went flying. The rest of the field managed to avoid a pileup and followed the Black under the wire. Ruskin struggled to his feet before the track attendants could reach him. The colt hobbled toward the finish line on his three good legs before collapsing tragically.

The videotape ended. Alec blinked. Seeing the accident in slow motion made it all the more gruesome. The TV announcer continued, "In one fateful moment the lives of two of California's finest Thoroughbreds came crashing to an end. Ruskin, an unbeaten young champion, the rising star of the racing world, had to be put down as he lay only yards from the finish line. Spin Doctor, another promising young colt, stumbled over Ruskin. When a postrace examination revealed irreversible spinal damage, he also had to be put down." Alec groaned. Not

Spin Doctor too! He'd half expected it, but somehow the news came as a shock. His heart sank a little deeper.

"Today's American Cup has already sent shock waves through the entire racing community," the commentator continued. "Here in California and all over the country racing will suffer from today's tragic events for years to come."

"Yeah. Sure it will," Alec said sarcastically. He switched off the TV. More likely, in a month or so the nation's horseplayers would forget all about both Spin Doctor and Ruskin. The fans would turn the page of their *Racing Form*, as they'd always done, to see another horse, another jockey and another race. In the racing game that's just the way it was.

CHAPTER 4

Spooked

A lec decided to take a walk. He needed to clear his head. A bag of carrots lay on the table by the door. On his way out Alec picked one up, broke it in half and slipped it into his jacket pocket.

The young jockey let his feet carry him where they would. He tried not to think about what had happened that day. But like a scratched record, his thoughts kept returning to the race...the dead horses...the jockey lying in the hospital. Get a grip on yourself, he thought. The Black won the race. You should be happy.

The familiar route he took led toward the Santa Anna stable area, only a few minutes' walk from the motel. The security guard recognized him and waved him through the gate. Alec walked down the well-lit shed rows and smelled the odors he loved...hay, ammonia and grain. His wandering ended at barn forty-one and the Black's stall, a roomy fifteen-by-twenty-foot cubicle.

Alec leaned through the opening and called softly to the Black. The stallion moved toward the half-doors. Alec took a piece of carrot from his pocket and held it out to his horse.

Watching the Black, Alec wondered what might have been the outcome of the Cup race if Ruskin hadn't fallen. Would the Black have been able to hold off the colt's spectacular stretch run? He'd never know now.

A few minutes later Alec stepped out into the night again. He walked to what had been Ruskin's barn. On a bench beside Ruskin's stall were a handful of oats and a neat stack of sugar cubes—gifts left in memory of the fallen colt by friends and admirers. Alec placed a piece of carrot with the other offerings.

For long moments he stared into the shadows beyond the open half-door, his mind filled with dark thoughts. Racing had changed in the past few years. Younger horses like Ruskin found themselves being pushed to go farther and faster than ever before. Lured by ever-larger purses, the owners and trainers competed under increased pressure to run their horses longer and harder.

This was not Henry Dailey's way, but that hardly mattered. When a horse went down during a race, it meant danger for everybody racing behind him. Spin Doctor was proof of that. Alec left the stable area and walked back to the Railbird. He remembered the empty stall, the offerings of oats and sugar. What a way to win a horse race, he thought. And what a waste of two fine horses.

→ → → → → ← ← ← ← ←

Habit woke him before sunup the next morning. He felt better. Any misgivings about what had happened yesterday were tucked safely away in the back of his mind. Hadn't the Black fought off Ruskin's charge down the backstretch and pulled up fit and strong? Sure, Alec told himself, the life of a racehorse could be a dangerous one. But if it was good enough for the likes of Man o' War and Secretariat, it should be good enough for the Black.

Soon he and Henry were at the track again, walking past rows of stalls in rows of barns. When they arrived at the Black's stall, Henry ordered a light workout, intended only to keep the stallion limber and loose. "Just open up his windpipe a bit," Henry said. He boosted Alec into the saddle.

The sound of the Black's metal shoes rang on the paths and paved roads that wound between the different barns. A security policeman stopped traffic so Alec and the Black could cross an access road leading out of the stable area.

The Black felt good beneath Alec, bouncing slightly when he walked. Alec came to the gap in the fence and turned right. A half-dozen horses were working out on the oval-shaped training track, running at different speeds. One and two at a time, they moved around the track counterclockwise. The exercise riders clucked to their mounts. Sometimes they shouted and called out to egg each other on.

The sun moved above the mountainous backdrop that cradled Santa Anna. Wisps of low fog and mist rose from

107239

the dew-moistened training track. The drumming of hooves filled the air.

A flagpole stood at the center of the infield of the training track. The sun crept higher in the east and the pole cast a long shadow, a line of darkness, halfway across the track. Alec had never noticed the shadow before. After what happened to Ruskin yesterday, it was hard not to.

Slowly the Black moved off after the other horses. No crowd of horseplayers cheered him on today. The area outside the track railing was empty except for the handful of trainers and early birds there to watch the morning workouts. Trainers punched their stopwatches as their colts paced each other around the course. One trainer followed his filly's workout using a palm-size video camcorder.

After a couple of lazy circuits Alec decided to give the Black his head and let him run at will for a turn or two. Alec moved the Black into the center of the track. The stallion took off at a sharp canter. His strides lengthened to a full gallop. Alec could feel his own heart begin to race. As the speed increased, time seemed to stand still. There was no past, no future. Alec belonged entirely to the Black. No room existed for anything else.

Ahead of him the thin line of darkness that fell from the flagpole became more defined. The shadow seemed to dig a gutter across the left side of the track. Images from yesterday's stretch drive flashed through Alec's mind, tightening his entire body. He could almost hear the crowd chanting "Rus-kin! Rus-kin!" The Black bore down on the shadow. Alec sensed a slight tremor, a shiver of twitching muscles.

Suddenly the stallion no longer responded to the reins. Before Alec knew what was happening the Black swerved hard to the right, avoiding the spot where the shadow fell across the inside of the track! He shook his head furiously and swung to the outside railing.

"Hey, hey, hey!" Alec shouted as the reins were wrenched through his hands. It took a long second or two for Alec to regain control. The Black slowed and snorted. Alec stood up in the stirrup irons. Wind-burned tears wet his cheeks as he leaned back in the saddle.

What happened to Alec and the Black did not escape the attention of the trainers and spectators watching the workouts, or the keen eyes of Henry Dailey. Alec rode over to where Henry was standing by the rail. "See that?" Alec asked, a look of bewilderment on his face.

"I saw it. What happened?"

"Don't know. He just took the bit and swung out. Wasn't a thing I could do."

Henry slipped between the fence rails and walked Alec and the Black to the point where the shadow fell. The old trainer took off his fedora and wiped his forehead with a handkerchief, the way he did when something was starting to bother him. The Black lowered his head to sniff and paw at the dark line on the ground.

"I don't like this, Alec." Henry's voice sounded serious. The Black bobbed his head impatiently. Henry stepped out of the way and tried to read the stallion's mood. He replaced his hat and turned to look up at Alec. "Try him again. Let him run with you this time."

Alec leaned forward in the saddle and set the Black in motion. Faster and faster he ran. The quadruple rhythm of his hooves thundered in Alec's ears. The Black's mane whipped his hands. Round one bend they flew, then the other. As the Black turned onto the stretch he switched leads to come on in full flight.

Alec tried to gauge the Black's speed—not quite a breeze, running close to all out, but plenty fast enough. He held the reins stiffly in his hands and drove hard along the inside rail. The shadow crossed the track directly ahead of them. At this speed the Black wouldn't have enough room to turn away.

Again Alec recalled yesterday's race and the drive into the shadow. Somehow he sensed that the Black was remembering that moment, too. Alec felt muscles tightening. Usually the Black ran for the joy of running. Now it felt forced, as if he didn't want to throw his legs down one in front of the other.

When the Black saw that he couldn't avoid the line of shadow, he simply hopped over it. Luckily the stallion landed in stride, never upsetting his internal rhythm. It was a dreadful replay of what happened yesterday to Ruskin, only the Black hadn't stumbled. If he had been going any faster…

The Black dropped his head toward his outstretched legs. His strides shortened and he slowed to a trot. Whatever overcame the Black as he approached the shadow, Alec could detect no sign of nervousness now.

Pulling the Black to a stop, Alec slid out of the saddle and looked silently over at Henry. The other trainers and spectators watched them as they left the track. Once out of earshot, Alec and Henry talked quietly.

"Seeing what happened to Ruskin yesterday must have really spooked him," Henry said.

"What'll we do now?"

Henry paused and scratched his chin thoughtfully. "I'm not sure, but the Black can't race again until we've figured this thing out and beat it."

Alec looked up at the Black. What was happening to his beloved horse? Overhead he heard the flapping of the flag. Whipped by the wind, it sounded like a taunting laugh.

→ **CHAPTER 5** ←

Trust Me

When they reached the stables, the familiar sights, sounds and smells no longer felt so comforting. Now Alec had a real problem, one he couldn't tuck away in some corner of his mind and ignore.

Alec and Henry led the Black to the walking path circling the barn. "Shadows have never bothered the Black," Alec said. "He's run through them a hundred times."

Lines of worry creased Henry's brow. "That was before yesterday's race."

"So what can we do about it?"

"Good question. Any horse but the Black, I'd try using a shadow roll when he races."

Alec frowned at the thought of adding the thick padded roll to the noseband on the Black's bridle. It functioned like blinkers and limited a horse's field of vision so that he couldn't see around his feet. "He'd never go for more tack on his face. Sometimes the Black still resents wearing a bridle. But there must be an answer somewhere."

Henry slapped his thigh angrily. "Jay-sus. If this don't beat all."

Alec tried to be optimistic. "Come on, Henry. Maybe the Black will get over this thing on his own."

"Yeah. Then again, maybe he won't. What then?"

Suddenly Henry snapped his fingers and his face brightened. "Hey! Wait a minute. I might know someone who could help us. I've told you about my friend Wes Taylor, haven't I?"

"The guy who trains horses for movies?"

"Yeah. He's terrific with offbeat problems like this. How about we let him take a look at the Black?" Henry didn't wait for Alec to answer. "His ranch isn't far. Let's give him a call."

Alec couldn't believe Henry was serious. "But we have to be at the airport in less than two hours! And what about the yearling sale?"

"I can take care of business at the sale by myself. You and the Black are going to see Wes Taylor."

"But..." Alec began. Henry ducked into the barn to find a telephone.

Alec stood there, feeling pulled in two directions at once. He'd heard all about Henry's friend, usually when they were watching some old Western on TV late at night. Henry seemed convinced that his pal had worked on practically every Western movie ever made. But how did that qualify him to work with the Black? On the other hand, a solution was needed. Somebody had to do something.

Alec continued walking his horse around the barn. Fifteen minutes later Henry returned. "It's all set. He's expecting you. And guess what? You know that Western series on channel 7, *Drover Days*? They have a TV crew shooting some scenes over at Wes's place right now. Paul Kramer is guest starring in a few episodes."

"Paul Kramer? He's still around?"

"Guess so. Remember him in those Singing Outlaw movies? They weren't half bad."

"That's great, Henry, but what about my horse?"

"Trust me, Alec. If anyone can help the Black, it's Wes. I've seen him work. He's really something."

Alec nosed the Black back into his stall just after eight o'clock, and in minutes he was driving Henry to the airport. Freeway traffic whizzed by. While Alec kept his eyes focused on the road in front of him, his thoughts returned to the Black.

It certainly would make things easy if Taylor had some quick, magical cure for the Black's fit of shadow shying. But if the condition persisted, they were in big trouble. The Black's racing career, perhaps even the survival of Hopeful Farm, hung in the balance.

Alec snapped out of his daydream just in time to make the airport exit. When they reached the departure area, Henry put a hand on Alec's shoulder. "Trust me, Alec," he said. "I really think Wes can help us with this shadow business. He's half horse himself." Then he grabbed his flight bag, waved good-bye to Alec and disappeared into the terminal.

By the time Alec got back to the track, all the other horsemen were packing up. Many had come to Santa Anna just for the races on Cup day. Now it was time to move on. Alec loaded the Black, and soon the top-heavy van was teetering back and forth on its way out of the stable area. Alec waved to the security guards posted at the gate. "Good luck," one of them called. After the bumpy road smoothed out, the van picked up speed. Before long Alec was cruising along in a steady stream of Sunday morning freeway traffic.

He wondered how Morales was doing in the hospital. A couple of spills like that could end a jockey's career. The thought made Alec feel uncomfortable. He wished he could get his mind off yesterday's race and everything that had happened since. It wasn't easy. He turned the radio on to distract his thoughts.

Soon the landscape changed from suburban sprawl to rolling hills. Wes Taylor's ranch was supposed to be about fifty or sixty miles from Santa Anna. After an hour on the road, the Black began to paw and scrape restlessly at the rubber matting covering the floor. Alec turned to look through the small window in the back of the cab. "I know, I know," he called sympathetically. "Just hang in there a little farther and we'll get you out of this tin can."

Alec dug a scrawled note out of his shirt pocket, the directions to Taylor Ranch. Somehow he managed to decipher Henry's handwriting and spotted the freeway exit for Sky View Terrace. Gas stations, fast-food restaurants and video stores lined the main street. Taylor Ranch was somewhere on the other side of the small town.

Alec turned west onto a freshly paved two-lane street empty of traffic. Ahead of him rose the shoulders of a high canyon. Bunch grass and thick weeds covered a gentle slope bordering the right side of the road. To the left were open fields.

The wide bottom land narrowed and steepened as Alec followed the road up toward the canyon. A billboard announced the approach to Sagebrush Village Estates, "A planned luxury community of the future." Large ranch-style homes dotted the terraced landscape. Spacious lawns, gardens and swimming pools surrounded each of them. In one area of the development bulldozers and backhoes were parked beside houses still under construction.

Past Sagebrush the road leveled off slightly. Acres of fenced-in pasture land replaced the luxury homes. Horses clustered together beneath shady oaks and grazed on patches of worn grass. Stately-looking Arabs mixed with compact Quarter Horses. A long dirt road bordered the far side of the pasture. This must be the place, Alec thought.

The paved road came to a dead end at a wooden barricade in front of him. Alec slowed the van to a crawl. He turned left off the pavement and drove through an open gate. A sign nailed to the gate read TAYLOR LIVESTOCK, INC.—LIVESTOCK, PROPS AND LOCATION SITE.

The dirt road ran straight ahead for nearly a hundred yards. It led past a ranch house, badly in need of paint, tucked among oak, pine and eucalyptus trees. A wide porch wrapped around two sides of the faded green building. The driveway ended beyond the house, where a number of small trucks were parked beneath the trees. Alec edged the van off to the side of the drive and pulled to a stop.

To the left, a dirt driveway split the ranch in two, running past horse pens and corrals. Alec saw no barns at all, just a cluster of small wooden buildings, most little more than sheds with aluminum roofs. Their Spanish-style design kept them open to the breezes, something possible only in a warm climate. This was hardly the Hollywood showplace Alec had imagined from all Henry had said about Wes Taylor. It looked more like a small working ranch.

Alec switched off the motor and climbed out of the van. A canopy of leaves rustled lazily overhead. A dozen or so people were working in a corral at the far end of the ranch. Alec wondered if Wes Taylor was with them. He walked up the dirt driveway to find out.

Henry had mentioned that a television crew was shooting some scenes for *Drover Days* at the ranch. This must be the crew. Some of them coiled thick black cables that snaked along the ground. Others folded metal stands and tripods or dismantled cameras.

"Hey there, young fella," a voice called from behind him. Alec turned as a man appeared at the ranch house door and waved him over. He was short, round and fifty-ish, wearing a red baseball cap and a long, soup-stained apron.

"Can I help you?" he asked, his voice reverberating with a Texas twang.

"I'm Alec Ramsay. Wes Taylor is supposed to be expecting me."

A flash of recognition sparked in the man's eyes. "Well, I'll be. I thought Wes was pulling my leg when he said you might be stopping by. Boy, that was some race yesterday! Saw it on the news last night. Too bad about the colt."

The man climbed down the porch steps and wiped his hand off on his apron. He gave Alec a firm handshake. "Jim Culpepper. Pleasure meeting you." He glanced over at the van. "The Black?"

Alec nodded. Jim's eyes widened. "How d'ya like that?" He shuffled to the back of the van and peeked over the rear half-doors. "Never thought I'd get a chance to see him."

Alec smiled proudly. Jim craned his neck, trying to get a closer look at the Black. After a moment he said, "I believe Wes's over in his schoolhouse. Come on, I'll show you."

Jim led Alec up the driveway. Just before reaching the crowded corral, Jim turned right. A narrow dirt path ran alongside the corral's split-rail fence. Midway along the fence they veered off on another path between more oaks and eucalyptus. In a clearing hidden among the trees stood something that looked like a huge wooden above-ground swimming pool. Rickety stairs ran along one part of the high wooden walls. A walkway rimmed the upper edge.

Alec had no idea what it was. The fifteen-foot walls kept him from seeing inside, but he could hear noises from within, a clattering sound mixed with a horse's blowing breath. It sounded as if the horse had just finished a heavy workout.

Jim pointed Alec toward the stairs and said, "Go on up. I best be getting back to the kitchen—or lunch'll be later than it already is." Jim turned to leave, and Alec thanked him for his help.

As Alec started slowly up the stairs, something heaved against the wall from inside. An unnerving squeal cut through the air. He reached the top of the stairs and looked down into the ring below. A big bay gelding cowered beside the wall. Hobbles made of thick rope ran from leg to leg and kept the horse from moving except to keep his balance. Nervous tremors rippled across the bay's coat, which was dark and slick with sweat. His ears lay flat against his head. Fear-widened eyes stared fixedly at the man standing before him—presumably Wes Taylor.

Taylor was lean as a wolf. He wore a stiff white cowboy hat and held a six-foot pole with a string of soda cans wired to the end. He shook the cans around the horse's head, then rubbed them on the horse's neck, back and legs. The sole purpose seemed to be to scare the hobbled horse out of his wits. Alec winced as the horse screamed again.

A minute passed before Taylor noticed the young man watching him from the overlook. Slowly he let the pole slide through his fingers to the ground. He squinted up at Alec.

"Looking for someone?"

"I'm Alec Ramsay. Henry Dailey said..."

"Ramsay? What do you know! How's Henry? I haven't seen that ol' horn toad in years. Is the Black with you?"

Alec hesitated before nodding. After what he'd just seen, he almost wished he hadn't brought the Black here at all.

"Great! Find Jim and he'll show you to one of the far corrals. The Black'll like it there, plenty of room. I'll be along soon as I finish up here." Taylor turned his attention back to the horse.

"What are you doing there, anyway?" Alec asked.

"Giving Salty Sam a confidence lesson. In here, a horse can't be distracted. The rattle of the cans gets him used to noise, makes him manageable on a film set. Some take to it better than others. This old boy'll come around." Wes cackled softly.

Alec climbed down the stairs. Could this old crackpot, with his soda cans, really be the renowned trainer Henry spoke of so highly? That sort of treatment might be all right for ranch or rodeo horses. It would never, never work with a high-strung animal like the Black.

→CHAPTER 6←

Rumors

Alec went to find Jim and then set about unloading the Black. Once out of the van the Black sniffed the air. His ears pitched forward, his eyes opened wide. Alec stroked the stallion's neck gently. Jim led the way up the driveway and followed the path running alongside the corral fence. It took them between some pine trees, then wound past more trees and back through the ranch property before ending at two empty corrals. One seemed about a quarter acre in area; the other was a bit smaller. Each had its own feed and water troughs. Sparse clumps of grass grew in splotches on the dusty ground.

On the far side of the corrals sprawled the green lawns and opulent homes of Sagebrush Village. A broken-down fence ran the length of the ranch property. It served as a boundary line separating the ranch from Sagebrush. Jim told Alec to take his pick of the two corrals. He gave Alec a little salute with his hand, then tramped back to the ranch house.

Alec opened the gate to the larger corral. Unclipping the lead line, he took a firm hold on the Black's halter. The Black uttered a muffled neigh. Alec stared up into the stallion's eyes for a moment, wishing he could understand the nature of the thing that troubled his horse.

"Don't worry, fella," Alec said. "We'll shake it." He only wished he could be as sure of that as he sounded. He gave the Black a clap on the neck and turned him loose.

The stallion charged across the corral. He zigzagged back and forth in short bursts of speed, then slid to a stop, throwing up a spray of dust. Lowering his bulk to the ground, the Black rolled over onto his back. The stallion kicked his feet in the air and grunted with pleasure. So much for this morning's careful grooming, Alec thought.

Alec filled the water trough and dumped the small bucket of oats Jim had given him into the feed trough. A few minutes later Wes Taylor drove up in a golf cart. Two long lash whips were propped up behind the seat like fishing poles. He still wore his white cowboy hat. The cart coasted to a quiet stop only a few yards from where Alec stood. The Black paced around the inside of the corral in lazy circles. Wes got out and walked to the fence rail.

A faint smile creased the old cowboy's leather-brown face. Piercing, deep-set eyes scrutinized the stallion's hind legs, ran along his quarters, then up the back, shoulders and neck. Finally he turned to Alec and said, "Now I know what's been keeping Henry back east all these years."

Wes's cheeks bulged with chewing tobacco. His drooping handlebar mustache was waxed and curled up at the ends. It made him look like a Texas sheriff in an old Western movie. He switched the chaw of tobacco from one side of his mouth to the other.

In an easy, drawling voice he said, "You know, every horseman carries around a picture of the perfect horse in his head. Never thought I'd see mine. But what's this little problem Henry mentioned?"

Little problem? Hadn't Henry told Wes about the seriousness of the situation? They were talking about something that could end the Black's racing career!

"This morning he started shying from shadows on the training track. It could mean big trouble for us if he keeps it up."

"What happened?"

"That's hard to say exactly. You heard about the race yesterday and Ruskin going down, didn't you?"

Wes nodded. "A real shame."

"It must have something to do with that. They were running nose to nose when Ruskin fell."

"Tell me more."

Alec recounted the events of yesterday and this morning. Wes listened, but his gaze seemed far away, as if he had something else on his mind. When Alec finished his story, Wes scratched his chin. "What's wrong with using a shadow roll?"

Alec shook his head. "That wouldn't work. The Black

is the sort of horse who has to see what's going on at his feet, even if it frightens him. Henry thought you might have some other ideas."

"Hmmm. We'll try a little experiment with the Black when we get back from the location shoot this afternoon. Right now let's get some eats. Hungry?"

"Sure."

Alec hadn't eaten much that day or the day before, for that matter. Lunch sounded great, but Alec wasn't so sure he liked the word *experiment*. The Black moved away from the fence to graze on clumps of dry grass. He seemed contented enough for the moment. Wes said he'd send one of his boys out to keep an eye on the Black while they ate. Alec just hoped whoever it was didn't try any experiments.

Before Alec had a chance to say anything, the old cowboy climbed into his cart and waved a fly swatter at Alec. "Get in. I'll take you on a little tour as we go along." They drove around the far side of the empty corral and then followed the boundary fence back toward the road.

"That's our neighbors over there," Wes said. "Some of those houses go for upward of half a million dollars. Used to be an avocado farm. Now they call it Sagebrush Village Estates." The way he said the words made it sound as if he wished Sagebrush were still an avocado farm.

Midway along the boundary fence, Wes pointed out a small cut stone and a well-tended patch of green grass. On the other side of the fence a bulldozer, like a sleeping dinosaur, sat beside a house under construction.

"Ever see *Lonesome Pine Territory*, Alec?" Wes asked.

"How about *Six Guns at Midnight*?"

Alec shook his head politely.

"No, I guess you're too young to remember those pictures. Guess I'm showing my age." He leaned out of the cart and spat a stream of tobacco juice. "Anyway, the hero's horse in those old Westerns was Sinbad, just about the greatest picture horse of all time. That's his grave over there. Sinbad helped build Taylor Ranch into what it is today. There'll never be another horse like him."

The cart turned left onto the main driveway dividing the ranch. The burned hulks of a truck and trailer sat off to the side, both charred black. Barely visible letters on the side of the truck spelled out O'HENRY'S CATERING SERVICE.

"See that?" Wes said. A sour look crossed his face. "Some idiot put gasoline in one of the diesel generators a couple days ago. It provided the electricity to the food truck and Kramer's trailer. When the generator caught fire, it burned them both up." So that accounted for the odor of burned metal, Alec thought.

"It was a real mess. Put us behind schedule and knocked O'Henry's out of commission for a few days. Jim's been filling in for them until they can get outfitted again."

They drove by the wide corral on the left. Wes nodded to the men inside. On the right was a lopsided shed housing two buckboard wagons and a hayloft. A small trailer, set on flattened tires, rusted beside the wagon shed. Alec learned later that the trailer was where Jim slept.

Past the trailer, and only about twenty yards from the

kitchen door, stood a well-maintained tack shed. Part of it had been converted into an office. Through an open doorway, Alec could see a work desk set up next to a lounge area of tables and chairs. Beyond the tack shed, the herd of horses grazed peacefully in the pasture fronting Lingo Canyon Road.

The light breeze began to carry a fresh scent, the smell of country cooking. Wes pulled the electric cart to a stop in front of the ranch house. Actors and film crew milled around, waiting for lunch to begin. Alec wondered if the famous Paul Kramer was among them.

At the edge of the crowd, a girl stood talking to a tough-looking, heavyset man in overalls. Wes walked over to them and Alec followed. The man's cap had the name BENBOW FEED COMPANY stitched to the front. The girl handed the man a check. "And tell ol' man Benbow that if you guys don't start getting the feed out here on time, this'll be the last check he sees from us. He's not the only supplier around."

The deliveryman took the check and snarled, "Listen up, girl. You people are still three months late on your payments as it is. You're lucky we came at all." He stuffed the check into his pocket and stormed off to his truck.

"This is my granddaughter, Ellie," Wes said proudly. "She's my right hand around here these days. And Ellie, I want you to meet Alec Ramsay."

She was about seventeen or eighteen, dressed in slim jeans and a loose work shirt. Her long, dark hair was pulled tight behind her head in a ponytail. She held a clipboard with a thick stack of papers pressed to it. Her blue eyes flashed as they connected with Alec.

"Hi," Alec said.

"So you're the one who rides the Black." Her tone of voice sounded mildly curious, nothing more. She didn't seem to be intimidated easily, or impressed, not by famous jockeys or hulking deliverymen.

Alec nodded. She was pretty enough to make Alec self-consciously straighten his shirt and run his hand through his hair. When she realized he was doing this for her, Ellie warmed a bit and gave him a smile.

"Pops told me he knew the Black's trainer. I thought he was just feeding me another one of his stories. He has some real gems, believe me."

Alec smiled back. "Thanks for the warning."

A phone rang inside the office and Ellie excused herself. Wes followed her, pointing Alec to the kitchen. "I want to see who this is. Go ahead and get yourself some eats."

Inside the kitchen, actors, production crew and wranglers lined up for their lunch. Jim hovered over an ancient stove. He dished up plates of beans and other vegetables and handed them out one at a time. Beside the stove was a counter cluttered with plates, an electric mixer and a can opener. Yellowing white wallpaper peeled from the ceiling. An oversize refrigerator wheezed plaintively in the corner.

The *Drover Days* crew on hand that day consisted of at least thirty people. The dining area of the kitchen was large enough to accommodate them all. Dozens of ladderback chairs surrounded three long, rectangular tables.

Plastic blue-and-white-checkered tablecloths covered each of them. Stacks of tortillas and biscuits steamed in straw baskets beside pitchers of iced tea.

The food line moved slowly ahead. In front of Alec waited two black-bearded young men. Light meters and camera lenses hung around their necks like medallions. Alec guessed they must be cameramen. They raised a forlorn chorus of "Beans again" as they picked up their plates. It was a good-natured protest and only half serious.

"Protein, boys, pure protein," Jim replied. "You're going to need it when you see what Frank's planned for you this afternoon."

Alec stepped forward and Jim handed him a plate of food. "Careful," Jim warned. "It's hot." Alec followed the two bearded men to a half-empty table. Technicians and carpenters, work belts slung around their waists, sat alongside a wrangler wearing a cowboy hat and an actor in makeup. Alec recognized the actor as one of the stars of *Drover Days*.

Alec had seen the show just a few times, usually when he'd been stuck in a hotel room near a track somewhere. It was a favorite of Henry's, about a gang of saddle tramps working their way across the old West and their adventures along the way. The good-looking horses and western scenery made up for the tired plots.

Alec eagerly dug into his food: bacon-flavored greens, beans, tortillas and hot biscuits. The room buzzed with shoptalk. Between mouthfuls Alec let his gaze wander. Ellie hustled from one table to the other, taking and delivering messages. When the phone rang again, she ran outside to answer it. She seemed to be constantly on the go. Obviously this wasn't much of a lunch break for her.

After Jim had served the last person in line, he came over and took a seat beside Alec. "The Black get settled in okay?"

"Just fine, thanks."

"He'll like it here after that madhouse at Santa Anna."

One of the bearded cameramen sitting beside Alec turned to his companion and said, "Wonder how much Jim is being paid to fill in for O'Henry?" He spoke loud enough to be sure that Jim overheard.

"Yeah," chimed in the other cameraman. "This is the second time we've had beans for lunch in three days. He's probably billing the production company for steaks, feeding us beans and pocketing the leftover cash."

"That's right, boys," Jim snapped back. "I'm saving up for a trip to Disneyland."

The cook and the cameramen joked back and forth. As they were bantering, Jim accidentally knocked over a salt shaker and spilled some salt onto the table. Reflexively, he picked up the shaker and tossed a dash of salt over his left shoulder.

One of the cameramen snickered. "Didn't know you were so superstitious, Jim. I noticed someone nailed a horseshoe over the porch door after the fire the other day."

Jim shrugged. "Can't hurt, especially the way things have been going around here lately."

"Hear anything new about how that fire started?"

"Nope. The generator guy still swears someone switched gas cans on him."

"But what about that lamp shorting out and exploding last week? Don't tell me you really think that was just bad luck too?"

The other conversations at the table tapered off for an uneasy moment of silence. The cameraman didn't seem to be joking around any longer.

"You mean the fire wasn't the only accident you've had here?" Alec asked. Some of the people chuckled.

Jim smiled. "Afraid not, Alec. But that's the nature of the business sometimes. Accidents happen."

"They certainly happen to us," said the other cameraman. "And old guys like Kramer, I don't know if they can take it. He really looked wiped out after his trailer caught fire."

"Kramer's not so old," said Jim. "Besides, that fire gave us *all* a scare."

A carpenter sitting at the other end of the table spoke up. "Think maybe someone torched the generator on purpose? Yesterday one of the grips told me that there's been a lot of friction between the producers and the Transport Union."

Jim picked up a spoon and shook it threateningly at the carpenter. "Where you been, son? That union beef was settled ages ago. You people should pay more attention to your jobs and less time spreading rumors around the set. If you did, we just might get through this shoot without any more surprises."

The first cameraman nodded toward the doorway.

"Just keep nailing up those horseshoes, Jim. I have a feeling we're going to need them."

Jim dismissed this comment with a grunt. He picked up a newspaper someone had left on the table and started thumbing through the sports pages. The others quietly resumed their conversations.

Alec stood up and took his plate to the sink. This was turning into one fine day, he thought. First the Black started balking at shadows. Then they had come to Taylor Ranch and met Wes Taylor, who acted like he learned horse training from Attila the Hun. And now Alec was hearing about some accidents that might not have been accidents at all.

He looked out the kitchen window to the horse van parked by the driveway. If things kept on the way they were going, he just might have to forget about this crazy idea of Henry's and bolt.

→ CHAPTER 7 ←

Tricks of the Trade

After lunch Alec took his glass of iced tea and went outside onto the porch. Wes leaned against the railing, a sleepy-looking black Labrador at his feet. Alec bent down to pet the dog. Wes nodded at the Lab. "That's Ziggy." Ziggy thumped his tail a few times but barely moved a muscle otherwise.

From inside his back pocket Wes pulled out a small, crumpled sack of chewing tobacco. He offered Alec a chaw. Alec shook his head.

"Henry still chew?"

"He quit years ago."

"Gonna have to quit myself one of these days, maybe when things settle down around here a little." Wes popped a wad of tobacco into the side of his mouth. "Guess it's time to get moving. Frank scheduled two scenes for this afternoon up in the canyon. One of 'em could be a real headache. He wants a herd of horses to run to a water hole on their own. I can drive you up to the location site with me. Or you can bring the Black and ride out with the rest of the boys."

Alec wasn't so sure he wanted to go along with these guys at all, especially after some of the things he'd just seen and heard. Then again, the Black loved rough, open country. Maybe a little exploring would do them both some good. "Think I'll ride out."

"Fine." Wes called to a broad-chested young cowboy standing by the tack shed. "Mike! Come here a second."

The cowboy strode up the porch steps toward them. He was about Alec's age but almost a foot taller. His arms and legs were long and muscular looking. Blond hair stuck out like straw from under a wide-brimmed cowboy hat that hid most of his face. A three-day beard shaded his chin, and a toothpick stuck out from the corner of his mouth.

"Take Alec here over to the little Air Stream out back and show him where to stow his gear, will you?"

Mike and Alec shook hands. After they collected Alec's bags from the horse van, the young cowboy led the way to a small silver trailer. So this was the Air Stream. It was just right for one person, even roomy enough for two if they didn't try to move around at the same time. Alec left his bag inside the door.

"How did you come to work for Wes?" Alec asked.

"I like working with horses."

"Not easy finding a job where you can do that any-more."

"Particularly if you want to eat regular."

Alec laughed. "I hear you."

"Most folks these days, you say mustang and they think you're talking about a convertible."

The blond cowboy told Alec that he'd grown up on a cattle ranch near Ojai, California. Ever since he was a kid he'd had a way with horses. A few years ago, after his father sold the ranch, Mike left home to follow the rodeo circuit. He picked up a job as a wrangler on a low-budget Western and met Wes. They kept in touch, and when Wes needed some extra help, he called Mike. Before long Mike started bunking at Taylor Ranch as well as working there.

"How about the other wranglers? Any of them live here?"

"Just me and Jim. Jim's lived with Wes for years."

"He's a cook?"

"More of a caretaker. He looks after the place when Wes has to go on the road. Lately he's been getting acting work. He played the part of a baseball manager in a beer commercial last week."

"You ever done any acting?" Alec asked. Mike was good-looking in a rugged, rebel sort of way.

Mike shook his head. "Nah. Acting's not for me. Stunts, that's what I like. But the Stuntman's Union is a tough one to break into." His eyes narrowed with determination. "My turn'll come."

The sound of neighing and whinnying came from the pasture. "The boys are saddling up," said Mike. "We'd better get going." They set off to collect their horses for the ride up into the canyon.

When Alec brought the Black in from his corral, he found Mike talking to two men in denim and cowboy hats. The taller one, with hair nearly as red as Alec's, crouched down to tighten the girth strap on his horse's saddle. The other, a short, dark-eyed Latino, gave Alec a slight nod.

Alec stuck out his hand. "Hi. I'm Alec Ramsay."

The Latino shook hands and flashed a toothy smile. "I'm Julio Garcia. Mike was just telling us about you." He jerked his thumb over his shoulder. "That's Patrick Rabain."

The big redhead stood up and pumped Alec's hand. "A real pleasure," he said with a smile. Alec smiled back.

Mike swung up into his saddle. "Okay, you guys. Let's get rolling."

Mike and the other wranglers escorted a dozen or so horses along the driveway: big Appaloosas, Standardbreds and Morgans. The wranglers themselves rode sturdy Quarter Horses colored chestnut, bay and roan. The Quarter Horses were built for speed and staying power, with broad, heavy hindquarters full all the way down to the hocks.

Turning left, Alec and the Black joined the wranglers as they set off for the *Drover Days* location site in the upper reaches of Lingo Canyon. The wranglers yipped and whistled, whooping it up as they rode herd on the unbridled horses. Their nimble Quarter Horses kept order easily.

The trail wound higher and higher, passing sloping granite walls and dusty boulders. Alec relaxed, letting his legs hang loose out of the stirrups. Riding with the wranglers, he felt like he could be living a scene right out of an old cowboy movie. He wondered what it would have been like to be a cowboy meandering along the dusty trail in the days of the old West. His gaze lingered on the dramatic-looking palisades, boulders and wind-twisted trees around them. No wonder this area attracted filmmakers.

The trail began to level off. Rounding a bend, it emptied into a box canyon hidden among the towering cliffs. The canyon floor spread into a wide plateau about a mile square. The crew had driven ahead of the herd in their Jeeps and four-wheel-drive trucks. They were already setting up at the location site, a small area lit by racks of powerful lights. A truck carrying a portable power generator parked a short distance away. Black cables snaked across the ground between the humming generator and the lighting, sound and video equipment.

Unlike the leisurely trail ride, the atmosphere around the location site felt charged with energy. The crew didn't walk; they ran. Men and women on ladders called back and forth as they adjusted camera tripods and stands of lights. With all the shouting and the noise of equipment being moved, the place sounded like a construction site.

Frank Meyer, the director, called out orders to the crew. Alec asked Mike what was on the agenda. "Two scenes," said Mike. "The first one should be simple—just some dialogue between two actors on horseback. The other scene is the problem."

Alec remembered that Wes had said something about a water-hole scene. He looked around but didn't see any water. Mike nodded to where Frank and Wes were marking a spot in the dirt. Four production assistants quickly began to dig a wide trench. A truck carrying tanks of water parked close by. As no water hole existed here, Mike explained, the art department was making one.

Mike popped a toothpick into his mouth. "The trick'll be getting the horses to run to the water."

"How is Wes going to do it?"

Mike shrugged. "Good question. There's no telling what'll happen if we just turn them loose up here. They might just lie down and take a nap. You can bet Wes has something up his sleeve, though."

"Mike!" Wes cried. "Stop jabbering and get your butt over here."

Mike hustled over to where Wes stood with the director. Alec felt a little embarrassed about getting Mike yelled at by his boss. He jumped down from his saddle and silently pledged to stay out of the way.

Wes, Mike and Frank huddled together for a moment. Then Mike and another wrangler mounted up and began moving the herd away from the location site to the far end of the box canyon. A white pickup truck followed; the words LOS ANGELES HUMANE COUNCIL were painted on its door.

The Black seemed to sense the excitement in the air and perked up his ears. Alec looked for a place to stand that would be out of the way but where he could still see the action. He found a spot behind and to one side of the camera. Alec turned around to see if they were in anyone's way. No one said anything to him.

Frank crouched down and peered through a camera lens. Wearing a long-billed cap with flaps covering the back of his neck and ears, he looked like an actor from an old movie about the French Foreign Legion. Now he backed up and moved from side to side, checking every possible camera angle.

"Places, everyone," he called, ordering the actors onto the set. One of the wranglers brought over a pair of Quarter Horses. The actors swung themselves into the saddles and took up their positions.

"Okay, you guys," Frank called to the actors. "I'll run down the situation again in case you've forgotten. The colt you're trying to break just threw Lefty here and ran off. Got it?"

"Sure, Frank. We're all set."

"Good." He nodded to the sound man, who flipped a switch on his console.

The assistant director spoke into a bullhorn. "Quiet on the set. We're rolling."

A production assistant stepped in front of the video camera holding a black slate clapboard. He read out the words on the slate for the benefit of the soundtrack. "*Drover Days*, episode 17, scene 7, take 1."

A puff of dust blew by and the Black snorted to clear his nostrils—disturbing the quiet. Alec clamped his hand across the stallion's nose.

"Action!" called the director. The actors twisted their faces into sneers.

"What's the matter, Lefty? Are you losing your touch?" taunted Jed.

"Let's see you try him on for size," Lefty replied.

Jed's horse shifted his weight from one leg to the other. The cameraman murmured something to the director. "Cut. Cut. Cut!" the director yelled. "Back it up, boys. Horse moved."

The action stopped and Wes stepped in to reposition the horse. After a moment the director called out, "Okay, let's take it from the top. Places, everyone. Roll tape."

The assistant with the slate stepped in again and read, "*Drover Days*, episode 17, scene 7, take 2."

"Action!" bellowed the director. The actors delivered their lines and the scene was completed successfully. But the director didn't want to take any chances. He reshot it three more times.

Alec yawned. He'd read about the tedious, time-consuming nature of film work. Now he believed it. Watching this scene being shot was like watching grass grow. He hoped the others would be a bit more exciting.

"What makes you choose one horse over another for a scene like this?" Alec asked Wes between takes.

"For dialogue? Sore legs."

"How's that?"

"A horse with sore legs will stand nice and still. All it takes to spoil a closeup is for a horse to shift his weight a little, like you just saw. A movement of half an inch can throw an actor's face into sidelight and ruin the shot." Wes turned his head and spat tobacco juice. "A horse that'll stay put for dialogue is a very valuable horse. And a horse with sore legs will stay put."

The dialogue scene took longer than Frank had

expected. Alec overheard the cameraman tell Frank that they were starting to lose daylight. Frank asked Wes when the herd would be ready for the next shot. Wes said he'd drive out to see for himself. Alec mounted the Black to ride after him.

A cloud of brown dust swirled over a small gully at the far end of the box canyon. As Alec came closer, he saw the wranglers running the herd in a dried streambed at the gully bottom. The effort spent jogging through the deep sand bore heavily on the horses. They were slathered with sweat and steaming from the heat of their own bodies. Their breath came hard and fast. Even the wranglers' saddle horses patrolling next to them looked worn out.

Wes was leaning against the hood of his Jeep, parked beside the gully. Next to him stood a man with a long hound-dog face. He wore a short-sleeve shirt and a necktie. The man didn't look very happy. He kept pointing at the horses and then to his watch.

As Alec dismounted, the man walked down into the gully. Wes motioned for Alec to come closer. "Frank wants the herd to run to water. I'll have 'em so thirsty they'll be able to smell a bucketful a mile away."

"I guess that's one way to do it," Alec admitted. Wes must have heard the concern in Alec's voice.

"Listen, son, with six weeks' advance notice, maybe I could have done things differently. But I didn't learn about this shot until yesterday morning. We're just lucky the wind is in the right direction to carry the scent."

Down in the gully, the herd labored clumsily through the sand. The man in the necktie stood watching them, a look of harsh disapproval stamped on his long face.

"Who's that guy?" asked Alec.

"Marty Fisher. He's a watchdog for the Humane Council. His job is to make sure the horses aren't mistreated. Some of their rules are a lot of nonsense. If a trainer knows what he's doing, like me, he won't have any trouble with them. But there's a lot of pressure to do things fast in this business. Truth is, every now and then a trainer will try to cut corners. One bum like that can give the whole profession a bad name."

The minutes passed slowly. Mike and the other two wranglers refused to let the herd slacken its pace. It made Alec uncomfortable just to watch them. Marty checked the time again and turned to face Wes. The look in the humane man's eyes said he would tolerate no more.

"Okay, Mike," Wes called out. "I think we're ready." Mike radioed the message to Frank on his walkie-talkie. "And tell him he better make it good," Wes added. "We're not going to get another shot at this today."

Frank radioed Wes that they needed five more minutes to get everything set up. In the meantime, Alec rode back to the location site. He wanted to see what the scene looked like from the camera's point of view. Finally Frank gave the okay and shouted, "Roll tape!"

On Wes's signal the wranglers started to chase the horses out of the gully and toward the water hole. They ran along with the herd for fifty yards or so. When the wranglers judged the scent had been caught, they veered off to the side. Their job was done.

The herd streaked across the sun-baked ground, zeroing in on the teasing scent of water. Sleek muscles swelled to push the pack faster and faster. No boot heels dug into their ribs. No bits pressed between their teeth. The unbridled horses were on their own.

Careening between rocks and cactus, the herd scrambled into camera range. The water hole waited for them, inviting and wet. The horses charged straight ahead. Two and three at a time, they plunged into the muddy pool. Some even lay down and rolled in it. Sheets of spray flew through the air as they shook the water from their coats. Alec could almost feel their relief. By the time it was all over, he wouldn't have minded jumping in there with them.

Frank kept the camera running while the horses played in the pool like a bunch of frisky yearlings. At last he called out, "Cut. That's a keeper."

The assistant director put the bullhorn to his lips and announced, "Okay, people. Let's pack it up."

"About time something went right around here," Frank grumbled. The crew gathered their equipment and started loading up for the ride down the canyon trail.

At last, Alec was beginning to understand the reasons for Wes's reputation as a trainer. Getting the horses to run to the water on their own was a neat trick, simple but effective. His methods might seem primitive, but they produced results. And he was far from the ogre he seemed to be at first. Maybe he really could cure the Black's shadow fear.

→ CHAPTER 8 ←

Ellie

The downhill ride out of the canyon took half as much time as the ride in. Alec turned the Black past a barricade, crossed the road and walked onto the ranch driveway. Wes was already there, waiting along one side of the drive by the fence. He waved Alec over.

"So now you see what I'm up against around here," he said. "Frank thinks I can rig a horse to do a stunt like some guys rig a car."

"He seemed happy enough with the way everything turned out," said Alec.

"You never can tell with directors. One minute they're happy. Next thing you know, they want to redo everything and add a helicopter shot. But now that we have a minute, let's get down to business. Aside from this shying from shadows, has the Black been behaving strangely at all?"

"No, he's been fine."

"Maybe what he ate for breakfast didn't agree with him, or maybe the weather?"

"Everything seemed normal as far as I could tell."

"You must have crossed through some shadows on the trail up the canyon. How'd he react?"

"Hmmm—I didn't notice. I guess he didn't react at all. On the trail or around the barn they don't seem to bother him. Anything resembling a racetrack is a different story."

"Think you could put the Black in motion over the length of the drive here? It's about the closest thing we have to a racetrack."

"Sure."

"Good. See that big eucalyptus by the driveway there, the shade falling across the middle of the lane? Try riding him into the shadow at a clip. If he turns out or jumps, go with him."

First Wes and Alec walked up and down the drive, checking for holes and stones. Then Alec brought the Black to the gate at the beginning of the driveway. The distance they had to run wasn't much more than a hundred yards, just long enough for the Black to settle into rhythm before they hit the shadow.

The Black edged across the driveway in a sideways crab-step. Alec leaned forward to rub the stallion's neck. "Don't be afraid," he whispered gently. "Nothing will hurt you."

Alec sat still for a moment and thought about what he planned to do. He had to keep the Black on track. It might help if he shifted his weight farther forward as they closed in on the shadow. Alec knew it was risky to put himself even more off balance. He decided to give it a try anyway.

Set in motion, the Black sprinted up the hard flat drive. The shadow came closer. Alec clenched the reins tightly and leaned forward. Within ten yards of the dark curtain, Alec got nervous. He could feel something disturb the flow of the Black's hoofbeats and break the supple rhythm. Alec flinched. The Black hopped over the line of shadow and came down hard. The landing threw Alec completely out of his saddle. It was a miracle that he managed to keep from being pitched off.

The Black continued on to the end of the drive. Despite what happened, Alec only murmured softly to his horse. There was no point in getting angry. Slowing the Black to a walk, Alec shifted back in his seat and loosened his grip on the reins. Now there could be no doubt, he thought. What happened on the training track wasn't an isolated incident. Alec rode over to Wes and dismounted by the pasture fence.

Wes looked the Black up and down. "If he was a green colt, I'd have a better idea what to do. But a seasoned racehorse suddenly acting up like this? That's not something you see every day."

"That's what Henry said. He was stumped and thought you could help. So what do you think?"

"Let me chew it over awhile and we'll see what happens tomorrow. Don't worry so much, Alec. We'll get a handle on this thing. But right now, you're going to have to excuse me."

"But don't you think..." Alec started to say. Wes had already begun walking back to the ranch house.

Alec stood in the middle of the driveway, stunned. That was it? "We'll see what happens tomorrow"? Why would the situation be any different then? Alec's disappointment turned to anger, most of it directed at himself. How had he talked himself into thinking that anyone could wave a magic wand and solve the Black's troubles? He felt like an idiot.

For the rest of the afternoon, Alec helped Mike, Patrick and Julio around the ranch. They fed and groomed the horses and replaced a few split rails along the pasture fence. Alec was more than glad to lend a hand. It kept him busy so he wouldn't have to keep worrying about the Black.

As the sun set, Patrick and Julio finished up their chores and went home and Mike headed into town to get something to eat. Alec tended to the Black and then walked over to see what was up at the ranch house. Wes met Alec at the porch door, welcoming him inside. The old cowboy led Alec through the kitchen and into the wood-paneled living room.

They sat down together on a brown leather couch to talk. Times were tough in the horse-racing business, Alec said. One horse farm after the other was going belly up. As they spoke, Wes watched Alec with cool, penetrating eyes. "Couldn't have hurt winning the American Cup yesterday."

"Sure. I think we'll get the prices we want for our yearlings at the sale. But I hated winning a race the way we did. And now look at what's happened to the Black."

"He'll be all right."

An awkward silence filled the room. Alec decided it was time to level with Wes. When he spoke again, his words carried the weight of his true emotions. "I can't tell you how helpless I feel about this. Nothing ever stopped the Black before. He loves to run. Usually he'll run through anything. This shadow business scares me."

Wes continued to eye Alec with that cool, penetrating gaze, as if he were figuring something out. "Try to quit worrying, son," he said. "It won't help. Besides, there's not much you can do to help the Black tonight."

For their dinner, Wes ordered a couple of pizzas delivered from town. Ellie was still working on some papers in the office. When the pizza arrived, Wes called her to come eat. She yelled back for them to go ahead and start without her.

After supper, Alec excused himself and stepped onto the porch.

A gust of cool wind blew by. Alec pulled his jacket closer to him. After a long walk around the ranch, he decided to check on his horse and took the path to the Black's corral. A lone figure sat on the top fence rail in the moonlight. As he drew closer Alec recognized Ellie. The Black was nowhere to be seen.

"Came out to have a talk with your friend," Ellie said when she saw him. "But he's hiding from me."

Alec whistled once, a long, low sound. Soon the black

stallion stood before them, silent and unmoving in the moonlight.

"Eerie the way he blends into the night like that," Ellie said. "No wonder I couldn't see him. He's beautiful."

"You must see plenty of nice-looking horses, living here."

"Nothing like him, though."

Alec let his eyes linger on the girl beside him. She was pretty good-looking herself. She seemed relaxed now, quite different from the person he'd seen answering phones and running errands during lunch. A ranch with two old men like Wes and Jim seemed like a funny place for a young woman to live. But Alec was hardly one to talk, spending as much time as he did with old Henry Dailey.

"How did you end up here, anyway? Where're your mom and dad?"

"They were killed in a car crash when I was little." Ellie spoke without lifting her gaze from the Black. "Pops and I went to put flowers on their graves the other day. We always do that around this time of year. Last week marked the fourteenth anniversary of the accident."

"I'm sorry."

"I hardly remember them. Never knew my grandmother, either. She died before I was born. Pops took care of me when I was growing up. Last year, after graduation, I started working at the ranch full-time."

"How's that been?"

"Crazy. I used to help take care of the horses. Now I spend ninety percent of my time doing office work."

"It sounds like what this place really needs is a secretary or an accountant. Why doesn't Wes hire someone to do the books?"

Ellie laughed. "Are you kidding? We could afford it if they'd work for free. We're so deep in debt it's pathetic. Just making it through this year will be a miracle."

Alec nodded. He knew how she felt. Recently he'd also been feeling a little overwhelmed by the business side of running Hopeful Farm. Yet Ellie's tale of woe made him realize how lucky he really was. At least Hopeful Farm could afford to hire an accountant.

"What exactly is your job here?"

"I guess you could say I'm the general manager. I keep track of things and make sure what needs to be done gets done."

"Sounds like a lot of responsibility."

"Tell me about it. I'd love to just work with the horses, like Pops and the guys. Can't think of a better job, if you can stand people spitting tobacco juice all over the place. But these days I feel like I'm practically chained to that desk."

They both became quiet. Alec watched the Black move away from the fence and disappear into the darkness. He forgot about everything they'd been talking about and thought of his horse. Ellie must have seen the concern showing on Alec's face. She touched his arm. "Don't worry, Alec. Pops told me about this shadow thing, and if anyone can help the Black, it's him."

They hopped down from the fence and started back toward the house. Ellie led the way through the trees and across the corridor. They stopped beside the field where the herd was pastured. Ellie pointed out a sleek Thoroughbred among the horses grouped there.

"Don't you think he's pretty? We call him Lowball, but his real name is Lord Bailiwick. Ever hear of him? He used to be a racehorse."

"Really? What's he doing here?"

"Kept throwing his riders. Pretty soon his trainer couldn't find a jockey willing to mount him. When we bought him, Pops figured out that Lowball was claustrophobic. Standing in a stall all day was driving him nuts. Pops cured him. Now he's Kramer's favorite mount. Gentle as an old mare, too, as long as he doesn't have four walls around him."

In the dim moonlight Alec could barely make out an exceptionally big Morgan standing off by himself. "Who's that?" Alec asked.

"Rex, named after Rex, King of the Wild Horses. The original Rex was a big animal star back in the days of Tom Mix and Gene Autry. Our Rex is a gelding like the others but still gets randy urges to herd and dominate—know what I mean?"

Alec nodded. "Some geldings are like that."

Ellie watched the Morgan move off into the darkness. "I doubt if there's a more rambunctious horse working in Hollywood these days. He thinks he owns this place. Never had a rider on his back. We put up with him because when a script calls for a wild-horse scene, Rex needs the least training to fit the part."

They left the pasture, made their way to the ranch

house and sat on the porch steps. Jim came outside holding the TV guide. "Guess who's starring in the early movie tonight? None other than our own Paul Kramer."

"As if we don't get to see enough of him these days. What is it?"

"Something called *The Last Bounty Hunter*."

"Think I'll pass on it, Jim. Those Singing Outlaw pictures were the only decent flicks Kramer ever made. Remember them, Alec?"

"Sure," Alec said. "Kramer was pretty good in those movies. I liked his sidekick, too. What was his name, Mc—something or other?"

"Hank McBride," Jim said.

"Didn't something happen to him? Some sort of accident?" Alec asked.

Jim nodded. "I'll tell you the story, if you want to hear. The real story, but don't go repeating it, especially around Kramer."

Ellie rolled her eyes. Alec guessed she'd heard this yarn before. The old-timer spun his chair around and straddled it like a horse.

"It was on the set of a movie called *Westward, Ho*. McBride and Kramer were playing scouts crossing the Colorado River on horseback ahead of a wagon train. The wagons were being floated across on rafts. Kramer fell off his horse and got swept downriver. McBride jumped in after him because he knew Kramer couldn't swim.

"Just then, some logs broke free of one of the rafts. McBride caught up to Kramer and pulled him over to the riverbank. Kramer scrambled up the bank to safety.

McBride wasn't so lucky. He slipped on the rocks and yelled for a hand. Our hero Kramer didn't even look back. Before McBride could hoist himself out of the way, a log slammed into him. It knocked him unconscious. He drowned.

"The studio kept the particulars about the accident hushed up. Bad publicity and all that. Afterward Kramer made a couple more films, but his career took a nosedive. Guess he started feeling guilty about not helping McBride. He started drinking on the job. His acting went to the dogs. Nobody would hire him until he got off the sauce. By then Westerns were in another slump. He was semiretired when the producers of *Drover Days* talked him into making a guest appearance on a couple of episodes."

"Now he's all ours, for better or worse," Ellie said.

"Kramer's not so bad. At least he's a pro."

"He still thinks he's God's gift to mankind."

"You'll see for yourself, Alec. He's due here in the morning."

→ **CHAPTER 9** ←

Visitors

A lcc left his trailer shortly before seven the next
morning. After grooming and feeding the Black,
he watched the stallion canter around the corral.
The stallion threw back his head. His long mane and
forelock whipped in the breeze. Alec's gaze lingered on
the refined features of the stallion's Arabian head, then
drifted to the slender neck with its high, mounting crest,
moved along the muscled withers to the strong back and
chest, the marvelously powerful shoulders and legs. Alec
knew the Black's features better than his own. Despite
this familiarity, he would never tire of simply perching on
a fence rail and watching his horse.

The Black stopped beside Alec, tossing his mane and
snorting defiantly. "That's it, fella," said Alec. "You tell
'em. Nothing's gonna scare you. Let's forget all about this
shadow nonsense, okay? This sure is the life. No Henry,

no workouts. Let's enjoy it while it lasts."

Though he'd been resisting it, Alec began to ponder what might happen if the Black really couldn't overcome his fear of shadows. It wouldn't be the end of the world if the Black had to quit racing. The Black could have a fine life at Hopeful Farm. If things worked out that way, perhaps it would be for the best. They might even find more time to travel together, to explore places they'd never been before.

Alec sighed. Who was he trying to kid? The Black still loved to race. When the Black wanted to start slowing down, Alec felt certain he would know it. Every fiber of his being told him that time hadn't come just yet. Some horses kept racing until they were eight years old, and the Black was only six.

Alec walked back toward the ranch house to find Wes or Ellie. A caravan of motor homes and trucks had already arrived to start work on *Drover Days*. Bumper to bumper, they jammed the space in front of the house and backed up out to the driveway. Among them was a brand-new food truck belonging to O'Henry's Catering Service. Actors and technicians crowded around a table spread with coffee and snacks, set up behind the food truck. Ellie was there, talking with Mike and Wes. She waved Alec over.

A door to one of the nearby trailers banged open and two men rushed outside. One of them was the director, Frank. Alec recognized the other, an athletic-looking man in his early fifties, as Paul Kramer.

"Looks like Frank and Kramer are going at it again,"

Ellie said, rolling her eyes.

"Kramer's been having problems with the scripts," Wes explained.

Ellie smiled knowingly. "And Frank's been having problems with Kramer." Mike just scowled and shook his head.

Kramer was ruggedly handsome, with broad shoulders, an iron jaw and a tanned face. An inch-long scar creased his left cheek, enhancing his tough-guy image. He'd been a country-and-western singer earlier in his career, then moved into acting in films. He fit the mold of a classic Hollywood cowboy, like John Wayne or Clint Eastwood.

Alec remembered Kramer best as the Singing Outlaw drafted into the job of small-town sheriff in the movies *Saddleburn* and *Saddleburn Two: Sundown at Cactus Ridge.* Kramer had made those films at least ten years ago. Except for some thickening at the waist, his physical appearance had changed little since then. In the flesh, he looked smaller than he did on-screen. He really wasn't much taller than Alec.

Last night Ellie had told Alec that Kramer was playing the part of the bronco-busting star of a Wild West show, Dallas Reed. In the story Dallas hires Jed and Lefty to help out with the show. Now Kramer held up the script and looked at it as if it was a dead fish that had begun to spoil. "Sure, I could deliver these lines. I could. But it would be all wrong. Dallas would never say them. It would be out of character for him."

"Sounds to me like you're just trying to make up for

the fact that you didn't learn your lines."

"Maybe I'd know them if they made any sense."

"Just deliver the lines, will you, Paul?"

Kramer sighed with exasperation and looked away. Frank walked off, and Kramer turned his attention to the service table.

Wes moved over so Kramer could reach the snack tray. "Frank sure can be a pain sometimes," Wes said.

"I can't work like this," Kramer grumbled under his breath. "What does he think I am, some kind of machine?"

Wes smiled. "I know what you mean. Sometimes I feel the same way about Frank." Wes introduced Kramer to Alec. As they shook hands, Kramer's expression was a mixture of distraction and disdain. It changed to a warm smile when Wes mentioned that Alec had just won the American Cup at Santa Anna. Kramer complimented Alec on his victory as he sampled a Danish pastry from the snack table.

"Mmm, these pastries are good," he said, smacking his lips. "Gonna have to put these on the menu—when I open my restaurant."

Kramer excused himself, saying he had to get over to the wardrobe trailer. Before leaving, he pocketed the last jelly doughnut on the service tray. One of the sound technicians nudged Wes with an elbow. "Heard the latest? Kramer thinks that somebody in the wardrobe department is shrinking his costume."

Ellie nodded toward the empty service tray. "I'd say he better lay off those jelly doughnuts."

One of the cameramen stuck out his stomach, threw back his head and did a fair imitation of an indignant Paul Kramer. "I can't work like this. I'm a ar-teest." Everyone had a good laugh at Kramer's expense.

Alec caught up to Wes on his way to the filming corral. "About the Black..." Alec started to say.

The old cowboy must have guessed what Alec had in mind and lifted his hand to silence him. "I know you're getting anxious, Alec. We'll do a little shadowboxing with the Black this afternoon."

Shadowboxing? Alec just shook his head. This was going to be some day.

By early afternoon the actors and crew had finished their work at the ranch, packed their equipment and left. Alec stood by the pasture gate and watched some of the horses as they chased one another, playing tag. Ellie came outside to join him just as a black Mercedes-Benz turned off the road out front and passed through the entrance to Taylor Ranch. The car was halfway down the driveway before Ellie noticed it. "Visitors," she called out. "Uh-oh. Looks like Rotasky."

Wes popped his head out of the office door. His eyes narrowed to slits as he watched the black car approach. Throwing the door open, he stormed out of the office and bolted past them into the house.

The Mercedes turned down the corridor and came to a stop in front of the porch. The driver stepped out. He was basketball-player tall and muscular looking. Long, stringy hair and mirror shades hid his face. He walked around the car and opened the rear door. A short, powerfully built man dressed in a blue suit emerged from the back seat. The man scowled as a cloud of dust kicked up by the car settled on his shiny brown wingtips.

"You know them?" Alec asked Ellie.

Ellie nodded. "They're from Sagebrush. The one in the suit is named Rotasky. He's the head honcho over there. The other guy is the company chauffeur. We're not on very neighborly terms these days. Ever since people started moving in over there, they've been complaining about something or other—the smell of manure, or the noise we make early in the morning, or the fence that divides our property needs repairing."

Ellie left Alec and walked over to meet the visitors. "May I help you, Mr. Rotasky?" she asked. Rotasky stepped forward. The driver folded his arms across his chest and smirked in the background.

"Ms. Taylor, I'm here on behalf of the Club Sagebrush Members Association. The noise produced by your film crew has brought about several complaints by residents. We've talked about this before. It's got to stop."

"Please let me explain…"

"If you people keep carrying on this way, we'll never sell the rest of our units. You're scaring off prospective buyers. I'm afraid this must serve as our last warning before—"

The screen door flew open. Wes came out onto the porch brandishing a double-barreled shotgun. He looked like a character out of an old Western. His face twisted into a menacing snarl.

"And I'm telling you one last time, Rotasky. I don't

give a damn about you and your prospective buyers."

Wes waved his shotgun in the air. A wild gleam sparkled in his eyes. "Get off my land. And take your goon with you. Go on. Git!"

Rotasky stared at the gun and back-stepped to the car, his legs trembling. "What the... Are you crazy?" he cried.

Ellie gasped. Diving past Alec, she ran up onto the porch. "Put that thing down!" she cried. She stepped in front of Wes and then pushed him back through the doorway. Rotasky took the opportunity to escape inside his car. The thug in the sunglasses ducked into the driver's seat and started the engine.

Ellie came outside and pulled the door closed behind her. Her face had turned slightly pale. Catching her breath, she stepped down off the porch. Rotasky lowered his window, keeping an eye on the kitchen door. "You'll be hearing from our lawyers about this, Ms. Taylor," he called. "That man should be in an institution."

Ellie called an apology after Rotasky. "Sorry, Mr. Rotasky. He's just been under a lot of..."

The black Mercedes spun its tires in the dirt and sped down the driveway. Wes poked his nose out the door. Ellie turned to him. "Are you trying to land yourself in jail or what?"

"Aw, it wasn't loaded. Besides, it ain't illegal to chase someone off your property. Damn Rotasky and his yard-proud tenants. Why don't they move back to Beverly Hills where they belong?"

Wes stepped toward his truck. "Okay, folks," he said. "I have to get over to the production office at the studio."

Ellie nodded to the house. "You're leaving the gun here, right?"

Wes gave a mischievous smile. "Of course. Want to come along, Alec?"

"I think I'll stay here. Thanks. Ah, about the Black..."

Wes raised his hand. "We'll get to it later."

"Later," echoed Alec. He couldn't help sounding disappointed. Once and for all, he wanted to know if Wes could help the Black.

Wes picked up a leather briefcase from the office and then walked out to his truck.

"Your grandfather do that often?" Alec asked Ellie after Wes left. "Pull guns on people?"

Ellie shook her head. "No, but then, he really can't stand it when Rotasky brings that chauffeur or bodyguard or whatever he is around here. That guy is just a thug."

They walked over to the porch and sat down.

"If you ask me," Ellie continued, "we're the ones who should be filing the complaint."

"How's that?"

"I don't think that generator fire was an accident."

"What are you saying? You think someone set it intentionally? Why'd anyone want to do that?"

"It's a long story. The bottom line is that we could lose our *Drover Days* contract if things keep screwing up around here. Without that money, we'd start missing loan payments and be forced to sell out. Rotasky would love that. He's trying to buy up the whole canyon."

Alec had suspected that there was more to the confrontation with Rotasky. "So you think someone from Sagebrush might want to sabotage *Drover Days* to get your contract canceled?"

Ellie nodded. "All I know is they're the ones who stand to gain the most if we go bust." They both turned and looked over toward Sagebrush Village.

"Talk to Wes about this?" Alec asked.

"Yeah. He says there's no proof that the fire wasn't an accident and I should forget about it."

"It's pretty hard to believe anyone would be so underhanded, not to mention criminal."

"Who knows what Rotasky might do to get what he wants? And if he's just a real estate salesman, why does he need a bodyguard?"

Alec thought about it. "Okay. Let's just say someone is trying to sabotage your contract with *Drover Days*. Besides Sagebrush, who else might want to make trouble for your grandfather? What about the union? At lunch yesterday one of the crew was saying—"

"Just an old rumor. That union business was resolved months ago." Ellie shook her head. "As if we don't have enough problems. We're just one check ahead of our creditors as it is. *Drover Days* is almost a week behind schedule. To top it off, the Humane Council has been getting on our backs ever since we took on this contract."

"Sounds like you have your hands full."

"And time is a luxury we can't afford."

Poor Ellie, Alec thought. She was desperate to pin the blame for the ranch's woes on someone. If their situation didn't improve, it sounded like Taylor Ranch would be out of business, or worse. Alec felt a sudden tinge of guilt. He'd been so wrapped up with the Black that he'd almost forgotten about anything else. For Ellie, the very survival of her home was at stake.

→ CHAPTER 10 ←

Breakthrough

A lec had just finished grooming the Black for the second time that day when he saw Wes come driving up the path in his golf cart. The cart glided to a stop by the corral gate. Wes motioned for Alec to join him.

"How'd things go in town?" Alec asked.

"I'll never figure out those desk jockeys in the front office," Wes grumbled. "Not only do they expect us to shoot a fight scene with a big buck deer tomorrow, but they still want to go ahead with this PSA the day after."

"PSA?"

"A public service announcement. This one is for a good cause and all, the Adopt-a-Mustang program, but we're way behind schedule on *Drover Days* as it is."

"So why do it?"

"A network time slot is already bought and paid for.

We have to have the spot ready in less than a week."

"Can't someone else shoot it?"

"Not really. The *Drover Days* producers volunteered our services for a reason. They want to patch up our differences with the Humane Council, and they think this is the way to do it. Marty's been complaining to the head of the studio. He's claiming the horses on *Drover Days* are being 'pushed too hard.' Ha!"

Alec could see where someone might get that impression about Wes. The old cowboy leaned out of the cart and spat out a stream of brown tobacco juice.

"The Humane Council is a powerful organization. If the complaints keep up, they could cause us a heap of trouble. Making this PSA might be one way to smooth things out with them."

Alec nodded. He had no idea the making of a TV show could be so complicated.

"Hollywood politics," Wes muttered. "I'll never get used to it." He snapped his fly swatter at a fly circling his head. "But enough of that. Tell me, how's the Black doing today?"

"He seems fine." They watched the Black prance around the corral for a few minutes. Then Wes told Alec to saddle the Black and bring him to the driveway so they could start their training session.

Now that the time for the appointment was finally here, Alec felt a little anxious. If Wes couldn't help the Black, what then? Wes watched Alec walk the stallion up and down the driveway. The Black's eyes darted about as he looked around warily. His nostrils dilated. He unleashed a piercing whistle through the air, a challenge to any and all who could hear it. The challenge went unanswered.

Along the driveway, a shadow fell beneath a towering eucalyptus. It spilled out onto the midpoint of the drive like a pool of ink. The stallion carefully avoided it as he passed by. It still seemed incredible to Alec that a mere shadow could have such an effect on the mighty Black. It was like a mouse frightening an elephant.

Alec walked the Black all the way out to the paved road before turning around again. He grabbed a fistful of mane and pulled himself up into the saddle. Wes gave a wave and Alec put the Black into motion.

Hoofbeats rang through the air, *ta-da-dum, ta-da-dum.* The tempo of triplets quickened to a rapid-fire drumming. Alec pressed himself down onto the Black's neck, blending their movements.

They charged up the long, straight stretch of driveway. Everything was as it should have been. For a moment, Alec thought the Black might not break stride as he bore down on the shadow. But then, a few paces away, Alec felt tension between himself and the Black. As he had yesterday, the stallion flinched and swerved sharply to the left. The sudden move came at the last possible instant and nearly threw Alec out of his stirrups. Only the strength in his thighs kept him from losing his seat entirely.

They tried again. Once more Alec wrapped himself up into the Black's mane. On this pass the stallion balked, breaking stride early and pulling up. Wes watched, leaning against the pasture fence and chewing his tobacco.

Alec rode over to Wes and then hopped down from the saddle.

"Maybe we should take a break," he said, as he put his hand on the Black's bridle.

Wes popped his fingers. "Hold up a second there, young fella," he said. "There's something familiar about this, and I just now remembered what it is. Water."

"Water?"

"That's right." Wes paused and switched his tobacco chaw from one cheek to the other. "Let me explain. Some time ago, a stuntman friend of mine was having a problem with one of his horses. Smokey was a first-rate stunt horse except for one thing—a fear of water. Even a mud puddle was enough to give him the heebie-jeebies. I got to thinking about it and figured we should try getting Smoke into a pool of water without him seeing it. Then he'd realize there was nothing to fear."

Alec burrowed his fingers into the Black's mane. "So what did you do, blindfold him?"

"Shoot, no. That would have scared him even more. We took Smoke to a shallow creek near Pete's property and backed him into it. It worked."

Alec saw what Wes was driving at. "And you think that's the way to go with the Black?"

Wes looked up at the stallion. "Only one way to find out." He motioned Alec toward the dark splotches of shadow falling across the drive. Alec led the Black to the edge of the shadow, then got up into the saddle.

"Okay, turn him around." Wes spoke with the easygoing confidence of someone used to giving orders and having those orders obeyed. Alec did as he was told.

"Now try backing him up, nice and slow."

Alec cued the Black to step back. The stallion hesitated a moment, then moved. Alec tensed in expectation of the reaction to this experiment. As the Black found himself surrounded by shadow he leapt forward, almost jerking the reins through Alec's hands.

"Let him go," ordered Wes. "Don't force him. He has to get over this thing on his own." Alec tried backing the Black under the shade trees again. Once more, when the shadow fell around the Black, he jumped out. Again they tried, and again.

Alec clucked and coaxed; the Black tugged on the reins. It became a game between them. Each time the Black stayed longer and longer in the shadow. Gradually, the rush to leave became less frantic. At last, he relented and stood quietly in the shadow without moving. Alec pressed his face close to the Black's head and whispered. "That's the way, big guy."

"So far, so good," Wes said. "Tomorrow we'll try again. If he cooperates, we'll lead him in headfirst."

"You're terrific, Wes. Thanks."

"Just remember two things, son. Patience and timing. Rush things and your horse will fall apart on you like a dime's worth of dirty ice. And remember. You're part of the equation, too. Take it easy. Relax."

Alec laughed. He wasn't the one with the shadow problem. "Me? You think I'm not relaxed?"

"You both look a little keyed up to me. Loosen up."

Alec smiled. "Whatever you say, Wes." The Black

tossed his head and neighed. This time, a chorus of whinnies answered from the neighboring pasture.

"Easy," soothed Alec. The stallion pawed and scraped at the ground. Dropping his head, he sniffed the area of shadow in front of his hooves.

After a short ride out on the road Alec took the Black back to his corral. He felt more positive than he had in days. This was the first sign that the shadow fear might be curable. Alec almost felt like celebrating.

That night Wes sent Mike into town to buy a bucket of fried chicken and biscuits for dinner. When Mike returned, Ellie stayed out in the office to work on the books. Obviously, the local fast food didn't appeal to her the way it did to Wes and Jim.

After the last piece of chicken had been gnawed to the bone, Wes, Jim, Mike and Alec all retired to the front porch. Wes asked Mike to check up on the horses and take a quick look around the ranch. Alec wanted to stretch his legs and went with him.

The air felt warm, quite different from the night before. Branches swayed in the hot, dry breeze that blew in from Sagebrush. Alec heard the light hum of cocktail music and garbled voices, punctuated by peals of giddy laughter. "Sounds like a party," he said.

"Yeah, every week or so they break out the Frank Sinatra records and really rock out."

They meandered along the fence toward the pasture gate. After double-checking the latch on the gate they walked up the path to the Black's corral. They stopped by the corral and leaned against the fence. Mike offered Alec a toothpick and the two of them chewed their toothpicks a moment in silence. Alec had something he wanted to ask Mike.

"Ellie thinks someone might have started that fire on purpose," said Alec.

Mike shrugged. "I heard. That idea sounds a little off the wall to me. But it doesn't surprise me, either. Ellie hasn't been herself lately."

"Really? How so?"

"For one thing, she doesn't seem to have time for anything but office work. We used to get into town for a movie every once in a while. Not anymore. Sometimes I think it addles her brains to sit at the desk in the office all day long."

"Maybe there's more to it than that. She told me that last week was the anniversary of the crash that killed her parents. That has to be on her mind, too."

"Could be, but Ellie was just a kid when her folks died. It's easier then." Mike spoke as if he were expressing fact, not opinion. "Have you ever lost someone you were really close to?"

Alec thought of Pam, someone he had lost. The thought of it was still painful, and he nodded. "Seems like just the other day."

"Then you know what I'm talking about. When you're a little older, when you're really counting on certain people being around to help show you what life is about and suddenly they're not there, that's tough."

"Yeah. Thinking about the way it could have been can drive you nuts."

Mike shook his head slowly. His features hardened. Alec wondered who the young wrangler had lost that was so close to him. Yet he didn't feel like pressing Mike for details. They were treading on very personal territory.

Back at the ranch house, Wes, Jim, Mike and Alec sat down for a game of cards on the porch. Wes ordered Ellie to put away her work and join them. "Quit being so antisocial, will you?" Wes said. "Alec's our guest. The work can wait till morning." Ellie sat down at the table, and Jim dealt her a hand of cards.

From out around the paddock the long, low hoot of an owl blew in from the trees. Ziggy didn't budge and lay quietly at Jim's feet. Ellie poked the dog gently with her foot. "Some watchdog you are," she scolded. "Where were you when we needed you?" Ziggy groaned and rolled over onto his back.

"You still think Rotasky might have had something to do with the fire?" Jim asked her.

"I just think—"

"Come on, Ellie," said Jim, dismissing her notion with a grunt and a wave of his hand. "There is absolutely nothing to suggest anything but an accident, much less that it was connected to Rotasky."

"I guess I just don't trust Rotasky and that creepy driver of his. If you ask me—"

This time Wes interrupted her. "Listen up, Miss Sherlock. You know how I feel about Rotasky. But you'd better think twice before you start accusing people of things you can't prove."

"That sounds pretty funny coming from you, old Mister Double Barrel."

"Yeah, well, never mind that."

Ellie just smiled. "Right, Pops."

Alec stood up from the table and went inside. He wanted to give Henry a call at Hopeful Farm and tell him the good news about the Black. Henry answered the phone and reported that everything was ready for the yearling sale. He asked if Wes was having any luck with the shadow shying. Alec told Henry about their small victory with the Black that afternoon.

Then Alec changed the subject. "I was thinking about how I'm supposed to get home. Have you talked to Cindy over at the travel agency?"

"Afraid I have some bad news in that department. There's a shortage of horse-plane space for some reason. Nothing's available till the weekend."

"You're kidding." Alec groaned. "I don't want Wes to feel I'm moving in here."

"He doesn't mind. I'm sure he's happy to have you."

"There's more, Henry. They had this accident here that makes me think…"

"What kind of accident?"

"A generator caught on fire the other day. Taylor's granddaughter suspects someone might have set it on purpose. Don't ask me why."

"Granddaughter, huh? I forgot about her. Is she pretty?"

"Come on, Henry. This is business."

Henry's voice chuckled over the telephone line.

"Relax, Alec. I'm just teasing."

"Wes is squabbling with the people he works with, his neighbors and just about everyone else in the whole state."

"Sounds like Wes, all right. But none of that has anything to do with you or the Black. Trust me, Alec. I'm sure the Black is as safe at Wes's ranch as he would be at Hopeful Farm. Besides, where else are you going to go? Must be pretty exciting around there. Have you met Paul Kramer?"

"Yeah. He's a real character."

"Give him my regards when you see him, will you?"

"Sure, Henry."

"I'll keep calling around for reservations and tell Cindy to check for any cancelations."

"Thanks."

Alec hung up the phone. After saying good night to Ellie, Wes and the others, he set off to his trailer. On his way there, he thought about what Henry had said. His old friend was probably right. What happened with *Drover Days* didn't have anything to do with the Black. Nor did it look as if Alec would be going home right away, either. Like it or not, he was to be a guest at Taylor Ranch a little while longer. He told himself that he might as well try to enjoy it.

→ CHAPTER 11 ←

Runaway

A lec slept peacefully, free from the nightmares that had haunted him for the past few nights. He got out of bed feeling refreshed, confident that yesterday's breakthrough would lead the Black to a full recovery. After grooming the Black and feeding him his morning oats, Alec set off to find Wes and Ellie.

Preparations were being made for the day's shooting in Lingo Canyon. The location site was the same one the director had used for the water-hole scene the other day: the little box canyon cradled in Lingo Canyon's upper reaches. The first scene would be a travel shot—Kramer driving a wagon at a gallop through the canyon. Louie Dousette, the actor who played Lefty, would be riding shotgun alongside Kramer. Frank wanted to get the camera in tight for the scene. He'd asked the actors themselves to drive the wagon instead of stunt doubles.

Wes pointed out the camera car that would be used for the job. It was an open Jeep with a custom-made mount rigged in back to steady the video camera. They would track alongside the wagon for closeups, pacing it at close range. Two pair of Appaloosas were to pull the wagon. Wes explained that the horses had been specially trained so the Jeep wouldn't frighten them. They were all tacked up and ready to go, dragging their long leather traces behind them.

The wranglers looked over the buckboard wagon one last time and then hitched up the horses. Soon the horses, wagon, Jeeps and wranglers set off on the trail up into the canyon. Marty Fisher followed them in his pickup.

When they reached the location, Kramer took his place in the driver's seat. He was stuffed into a spotless white leather cowboy outfit. His longish brown hair was carefully groomed, mussed to perfection where it bristled out from under his white cowboy hat. Beside him, Dousette wore his standard cowboy gear: boots, jeans, a black denim jacket and a wide-brimmed hat. Frank had again donned his flapped cap and sunglasses for the occasion. The Foreign Legion has arrived, Alec said to himself.

The director looked Dousette up and down. "What's with that hat, Louie? It looks like you just bought it. You're supposed to be coming back from a three-day trail ride, remember?" He plucked the hat off the actor's head and crumpled the brim. Then he mashed it some more, and replaced it on Dousette's head. The actor smiled stoically. Frank stepped back to admire his handiwork. "Much better," he concluded.

Frank turned to Kramer. "Okay, Paul. This should be simple, so we'll try it without a run-through. You ready?"

"Relax, Frank," Kramer said, reaching for the lines. "I was driving wagons when you were still in film school, remember?"

"You know the route. Just keep to it."

Frank, the cameraman and an assistant positioned themselves in the back of the camera car behind the driver. Wes followed after them in his own Jeep. Alec and the Black rode along with the wranglers, who waited on their pickup horses just out of camera range. Their job was to chase and help stop the wagon at the end of its run.

"Action!" shouted the director. Kramer shook the reins and the horses stepped off at a slow trot. The camera car drove beside the wagon, keeping Kramer in focus. He cracked his lash whip loudly in the air. The two teams picked up speed.

At first everything went as planned. The camera crew got the shot they needed, and the director yelled, "Cut!" The car veered away and slowed down. But when Kramer yanked on the lines to pull up the team, there was no response from the horses. First one rein, then the other, slackened in his hands. Something had broken. The horses were running out of control!

The wagon continued to accelerate. Dousette hung on desperately to his seat. Kramer dropped the reins and clambered into the back of the wagon.

The horses were panicking, running much too fast for the actors to jump out. That might not have been so bad if they had kept to their route. But directly in the wagon's path loomed a stand of tall oak trees. The oaks were the only trees in the entire canyon, and the stand was the only place that the team should have avoided. The wagon headed straight for it.

The two lead horses fought each other for control of the wagon as they closed in on the trees. One horse struggled to turn left, the other pulled to the right. Neither was strong enough to overcome the other. Nor was there any possibility of slowing down or stopping as the frightened wheel team behind them pushed faster and faster.

Alec watched in horror as the out-of-control horses drove headlong toward the trees. The wranglers charged after them, but it quickly became clear that only Mike might be close enough to reach them in time.

Mike's speedy little pinto Quarter Horse caught up to the runaway wagon and came alongside the lead team on the right. Tugging at the lead horse's bridle, shouting and whistling, Mike did everything he could to stop the team, short of falling down in front of them. But try as he might, he couldn't turn or slow the wagon. The horses bore down steadily on the stand of trees.

There were only a few seconds left in which to act. Frantically Mike made one last, heroic attempt to turn the wagon. He jumped from his saddle onto one of the lead horses. Bouncing across the horse's back, he grappled with the bridle and tried to pull back the horse's head. Still the team refused to change direction. At the last possible instant, Mike leapt away from the wagon. He saved himself by tucking into a ball and rolling when he hit the ground.

With an awful whack, the horses crashed into the narrowly spaced tree trunks. They were running at a full gallop when they hit. The wagon slid sideways, overturned and smashed apart. Kramer and Dousette went flying through the air. The horses piled into one another and then thudded to the ground.

Before the dust settled, Alec and the wranglers got to the crash scene. Broken pieces of wagon lay strewn about. A wheel spun in the air, wobbling on its broken axle. Bodies sprawled on the ground. Patrick and Julio dismounted on the run and rushed from one victim to the other.

Alec tended to the wranglers' horses. He led them to the far side of the stand of trees and looped the ends of their reins around a low-hanging branch. The Black looked around warily. After a few soft words to calm the stallion, Alec ran over to help the others.

Though obviously shaken up, both Mike and Kramer seemed unhurt. Dousette wasn't so lucky. The young actor lay on his back, unconscious. Patrick stopped Julio from trying to move him. "We'd better wait until we get help. I'll stay here. You two see about the horses."

From the look of things, only one of the Appaloosas, Pal Joey, had taken the full brunt of the impact into the trees. He lay on the ground mortally wounded, his head split open and oozing gore. The other horses struggled to get up. The sound of their frantic whinnying sent a chill through Alec.

While Alec knelt beside Joey to hold him still, Julio freed the rest of the team from their tangled harness. The horses staggered to their feet. Cuts and scrapes marked their legs and shoulders. Miraculously, they seemed to have escaped the crash without any major cuts or broken bones.

Alec couldn't bear looking at Joey's wound. He turned his head away. Horrible grunts and groans rasped from Joey's throat. Alec's hands began to shake.

Wes was in the first Jeep to arrive, even before the camera car. He ran over to the fallen horse. On seeing the sickening head injury, he must have known immediately that Joey would never survive. There was only one thing that could be done. Wes fumbled in his pocket for a folding knife. A flash of metal shone in his hand. The old trainer knelt beside the injured horse and jerked the knife across the horse's throat. In a moment Joey lay still.

Wes stood up slowly. Blood dripped from the jackknife in his hand. Alec pulled himself to his feet. He felt weak in the knees. His hands still trembled, and he stuffed them into his pockets. Hadn't he been here before? This was the second fatal accident he'd witnessed in three days. Vomit suddenly choked his throat. He ran behind a tree and was sick.

CHAPTER 12

Sabotage

The next Jeep to reach the crash site was the camera car. Frank jumped out, quickly checked on the actors and then stormed over to Wes. He took off his French Foreign Legion cap and threw it to the ground. His face was red and veins stood out on his forehead. "Two days ago we lost the trailer. Today this. What's with these animals of yours?"

"Don't start up with me, Frank. You know I can't program a horse like a computer. They have minds of their own."

"And you're paid to train them, right? These setbacks are going to finish us. We've lost Kramer and Dousette for the rest of the day at least."

"That's not all we lost," Wes said quietly.

"We're lucky someone didn't get killed, instead of just a horse," the director said.

Wes squinted his eyes and leveled a cool stare at the director. He bent down to pick up a lash whip that had fallen from the wagon and lay on the ground nearby.

"Just a horse, huh, Frank? Just a horse? Why, I've half a mind to..." He snapped the whip with deadly accuracy, popping the dirt inches from the director's feet.

Frank jumped backward. "You crazy carny. Are you *trying* to lose this job or what?"

Wes loosened his hold on the whip and let it slide through his hands to the ground. He looked down at the dead horse and took a deep breath. His voice softened. "Someone has to take care of these horses, Frank. You want to do it?"

Frank didn't say anything.

"Leave me be, will you, Frank? I have work to do. Go on now."

"Okay, Taylor. We'll talk about this later." Frank spun around and marched back to the camera car.

Alec walked over to check on the Black. His stomach still felt a little queasy. On the other side of the trees the wranglers' Quarter Horses bunched together with the Appaloosas. Steam rose from their sweat-drenched coats. Some of them started running up against each other. They must have smelled the death in the air. Alec caught hold of the Black's bridle. He moved the stallion upwind and away from the others.

Kramer sat on the ground near Alec, rubbing his shoulder and moaning loudly. Considering what had just happened, the actor had been incredibly lucky. He'd slid at least twenty yards across the dirt, but his leather suit had protected him from being hurt. Now Alec understood why motorcyclists wore leather outfits. One of the cameramen knelt beside him. "How are you feeling, Paul?"

"I'm getting too old for this."

"Everything's going to be all right. We'll get you out of here as soon as the rest of the crew shows up. You just hang in there."

The other Jeeps arrived, and the rest of the crew pitched in to help. The injured actor, Louie Dousette, was carried to a Jeep and driven back to the ranch. Alec overheard someone say that the actor would have to go to the hospital.

It didn't take long for Kramer to begin playing the part of the tough old trooper. "This is nothing," he said. "Why, you people shoulda seen what happened to me on the set of *Texas Territory*." He shared his story with the three crewmen who helped him to his feet and escorted him to another Jeep.

When Marty Fisher reached the crash site, he rushed straight over to Wes, who still stood beside the fallen horse. Marty shook his head with disgust. "For crying out loud, Taylor."

"Would you've rather I waited for a vet? Anyone could see Joey wasn't gonna make it."

"So you had to cut his throat with a jackknife?"

"What else was there?"

The scowl on Marty's face deepened to a dark frown. "You know I'm going to have to report this. The council might want to bring charges." Wes nodded.

The humane man's anger was understandable, Alec thought. After all, his job was to look out for the horses' welfare. Yet he must have seen what Wes meant. Waiting for a vet to put Joey down could have taken hours. Someone needed to act. Wes took the responsibility and did what had to be done.

Mike came limping by in a daze. He looked badly shaken, even if he hadn't broken anything. No one could jump from a horse at that speed without getting bruised. Patrick tried to get Mike into a Jeep so he could be driven back to the ranch.

"I almost had 'em," Mike said. "Just another second and..."

Patrick put his arm around Mike's shoulders. "Don't feel too bad, Mike. You tried. And I'm sure Kramer appreciates what you did."

Mike shrugged off the consoling arm and staggered away. "Kramer!" he said. "Man, I was thinking about the team, not that dude."

Wes chased after Mike. "If you won't go to the hospital," he said, "at least go back to your trailer and lie down. That's an order, Mike." The wrangler did as he was told and climbed into the back of the camera car.

Frank gave the word to cancel work for the rest of the day and headed back to the ranch.

Marty pulled out a notebook and began making notes for a report to the Humane Council. He talked with the wranglers and looked over the wagon and harness. After finishing the notes for his report, Marty also got back into his truck and left.

The wranglers, Alec and Wes stayed behind to take care of burying Joey. They dug a grave a short distance from where the poor Appaloosa had fallen. Wes, deeply shaken, kept looking at the shattered wagon, as if staring at it long enough would somehow reveal how this could have happened.

Alec turned the Black out with the other horses, who were looking for patches of dry grass among the tumbleweeds and yucca plants dotting the landscape. Clouds moved over the sun, shrouding the canyon. Gloom seemed to hang in the air even after the sun burned through the clouds again.

Alec watched Patrick and Julio tamp down the last few shovelfuls of earth over Joey's grave. Patrick jammed the shovel into the dirt. "Joey was a good old boy. Always worked hard, did what you told him. Doesn't seem right it should end like this for him."

Julio shook his head. "I hear you."

"I still can't figure how those lines busted like that. They weren't more than a month old."

"Only been used two or three times at the most."

Alec also wondered about the broken lines, and he wondered what the other two were thinking. He turned to Patrick. "What happened to them, anyway? Did they just rip apart or what?"

Patrick shrugged. "Who knows? Cheap leather, maybe something else. Man, that was some crackup."

Julio nodded in agreement. "*Aye, hombre.* I wonder how Mike is feeling after that fall. He went flying!"

"He didn't seem to be hurt too bad."

"Lucky guy."

They stood there in silence for a moment and looked down at the grave. Then Patrick touched the brim of his cap in a salute. "Good-bye, old fella."

Julio crossed himself and rubbed his foot through the dirt. "*Adiós, amigo.*" The two wranglers shouldered their rakes and shovels and carried them back to the Jeep. Alec followed after them.

Alec heard the sound of a Jeep coming up the trail. The Jeep drove out into the box canyon. It came closer and parked near the overturned wagon. Ellie got out and ran over to Wes.

Alec guessed she had heard what had happened from the crew. He wondered what Ellie thought about it all. Before the wagon crash, he'd been inclined to doubt her suspicions of sabotage on *Drover Days.* Now he wasn't so sure.

Everyone gathered beside the wagon. Wes fingered the frayed ends of the two broken harness lines. Ellie stood back from the others, and her intense gaze shifted between Wes and the lines.

Patrick and Julio crowded around to get a better look at the pieces of broken leather. Their voices hushed to whispers as the lines were passed from hand to hand.

"Will you look at that?"

"Well, I'll be."

When the reins reached her, Ellie took a close look at the torn strips of leather. She shook her head and handed the lines to Alec. He ran his fingers over the leather.

Alec pointed to the frayed stitches. "It just looks worn through," he said.

"Yeah, almost too worn, as if someone distressed the leather on purpose," she said.

"You mean someone scuffed it up just to make it look worn out?"

Ellie nodded. "When I worked in wardrobe one summer, we did it all the time. It's easy to make new things look old."

She pointed out a two-inch-long section on either side of the broken line. "See there? It could have been cut apart and then loosely sewn back together, like a prop that's supposed to break." Alec saw that some of the stitches were split cleanly in half. Only a sharp knife or razor could have made such a cut.

Wes frowned. "I should have caught it. I should have checked out the wagon and tack this morning."

"Don't start blaming yourself, Wes," said Patrick. "What happened to Joey wasn't your fault." Julio nodded in agreement.

"Maybe not, but Ellie has a point. Those stitches look cut. Anyone can see that. It looks like someone set us up."

"So what are we going to do about it?" asked Ellie.

"For one thing, I'm going to call the sheriff as soon as we get back home. Maybe he can figure this thing out for us."

Everyone started back to the ranch. Alec boosted himself up onto the Black and started to the head of the trail. Ellie was right, he thought. It looked like someone wanted to stop *Drover Days* and didn't care who got hurt in the process.

The wagon crash wasn't some harmless prank. It had left a horse dead, a wagon destroyed and sent at least one actor on his way to the hospital. Yet even with the reins as evidence, they weren't any closer to finding out who was behind the sabotage than they were before the accident.

Alec squeezed his legs and pressed the Black into a gallop. He needed to lose himself in that familiar surge of speed, let the rush of wind in his face clear his mind. The thunder of hoofbeats filled his ears. He felt nothing but the oneness with his horse. For a few brief seconds, everything else was swept away.

→CHAPTER 13←

A Helping
Hand

Alec left the Black in his corral. He walked over to
the house and sat on the porch steps. The ranch,
which had looked like a crowded parking lot earlier that morning, was quiet again. Ellie came out of the
office and called to Alec, "Let's go see how Mike's doing.
I'm a little worried about him."

Ellie gave a rap on the door to Mike's trailer and
walked inside. Mike was stretched out in bed. He sat up,
glanced at his visitors, then reached down to adjust an
ice pack wrapped around his left ankle.

"How you feeling, Mike?"

"I'll be all right."

Ellie sat down on the edge of the bed. Picking up the
ice pack, she poked at Mike's swollen ankle.

"Ouch!"

"Sure you don't want to see a doctor about that?"

"Nope. I wouldn't even be in here if Wes hadn't ordered me to."

"Well, nothing's happening, anyway. Frank moved the crew to the studio for the rest of the day."

"How'd the other horses in the team make out?"

"The vet's coming over later to take a look. They seem okay. But we don't know about Dousette yet. He's still at the hospital."

"What happened to Kramer?"

"Oh, he's fine and dandy. Just a few scrapes. Kramer must be the luckiest guy in all of Hollywood. I doubt that he'll be up for any barrel riding for a few days, though."

As Ellie and Mike talked, Alec looked around the room. Mike's trailer was small, about the same size as Alec's. Every square inch of wall space was papered with publicity stills and cutouts from movie and horse magazines. On a shelf by the window were a half-dozen gold- and silver-plated belt buckles, trophies won for bronc riding, roping and other rodeo events. A movie poster from the John Wayne Western *Stagecoach* hung on the back of the door.

Among the pictures Alec noticed a fading, dog-eared photo clipped from a newspaper. There was no caption beneath the photo, but it appeared to be Mike receiving a trophy at a rodeo. Alec recognized something familiar about the guy in the floppy hat presenting the trophy but couldn't quite place him.

The front door opened and Jim poked his nose inside. "Howdy, Mike. You feeling better?"

Mike gave him a sidelong glance. "Hey, what is this, open house?"

"Just came to see if there's anything I could do."

Mike muttered something under his breath. Ellie took the hint. It seemed that they'd overstayed their welcome. "Sorry, Mike. We'll leave you be." She shooed Jim away and closed the door behind them.

"He seems all right," Alec said.

Ellie nodded. "Mike's funny sometimes. You never can tell what he's really thinking. He always has to play the tough guy, the hero."

Jim thumped his chest. "I'd of done what he did myself if I could have."

Ellie smiled and nudged Alec. "Sure you would, Jim."

Jim's face lit up with anger and pride. "You doubt it? I'm not that old, missy. I'd put myself on the line for this place any day of the week."

Ellie's voice gentled. "We know you would, Jim."

Alec saw Wes sitting on a bench outside the doorway to the tack room. The old cowboy waved them over. He looked tired. New lines of worry marked his face. He'd just finished speaking on the phone with someone at the hospital. Dousette was still unconscious.

Jim scratched his chin. "Poor Louie. Funny the way Kramer's partners end up taking the fall when things get tough. Kramer always manages to scrape by, though."

Wes nodded. "We're just lucky Kramer's still in one piece after that wagon crackup. At least he'll be able to be around for that PSA. But without Dousette, I don't know how we're going to pull it off."

"His part wasn't that tough, was it?"

"No, but even so, I don't know who we can get to fill in for him on such short notice."

Ellie shook her head. "At this point, I wonder if it'll make any difference. After what happened to Joey, it just might be too late to smooth things out with the Humane Council."

A black-and-white police cruiser turned off the road out front. Jim turned to watch it. "What's O'Brien doing here?" Wes told him about finding the cut stitches in the wagon harness.

Jim didn't believe any of it. "What!" he bellowed. "You guys really think someone could have snuck into the tack room and messed around with the tack right under our noses?"

"I'm not accusing anyone," Wes said, shrugging, "just being careful."

"Come on."

"Take off the blinkers, Jim. Some people will do whatever it takes to get ahead. For them, it's hooray for me and the heck with the other guy. You're too trusting."

"And you're crazy to be buying into Ellie's conspiracy theory."

The patrol car rumbled up the driveway and pulled to a stop in a cloud of dust. SKY VIEW TERRACE POLICE was printed on the car door. Sheriff Nick O'Brien, a husky, middle-aged man, got out and slammed the car door behind him.

Wes strode over to greet him. "Thanks for coming, Nick." The police officer shook Wes's hand and then casually adjusted the thick, black leather gun belt slung around his waist. Wes led the way into the tack room and showed O'Brien the harness, pointing out the spot where the lines had broken.

"Horses are your department, Wes," the policeman said. "I wouldn't know one harness from another." O'Brien put the harness down. His tone of voice evened, all business. "So let's have it. What's this all about?"

Wes took a deep breath. He told O'Brien the whole story. The officer listened quietly, scribbling notes onto a pad of paper.

When Wes had finished, O'Brien put down his pencil. "What took you so long to report that fire?"

"Up to now, we weren't sure it was anything more than bad luck."

"From what you've said, that might be all it is. But you did the right thing in giving me a call. Can you think of anyone who might have a grudge against you?"

"This is a competitive business, and I've been in it for more than thirty years. I'm sure I've stepped on some toes along the way."

"Anything might help, no matter how unimportant it may seem to you."

Ellie, who up to this moment had been listening quietly, told the sheriff about her suspicions of Sagebrush.

The sheriff asked about the people working on *Drover Days*. Wes told him that the makeup of the cast and crew was determined by the type of shots planned for the day. Some days there were only a handful of people working at the ranch; other times there might be thirty or forty.

"I think you're all way off base with this sabotage business," said Jim, "but if you want to know someone with a grudge against us, well, what about Emerson Livestock? They're our main competition. Tell you what, those guys weren't very happy when we won the *Drover Days* contract away from them."

Wes chuckled at Jim's suggestion. "I reckon not. Still, I can't believe anyone at Emerson's would sabotage one of our wagons."

"I can't either," Jim admitted, "but the sheriff said he wanted to know of anything, no matter how far-fetched."

"That's pretty far-fetched, all right."

"Then I guess you don't want to know who I saw talking with the foreman from Emerson's Ranch at the pizza parlor in town the other day."

"Who?"

Jim swallowed and turned his head, looking slightly ashamed of what he was thinking. "Julio."

Wes frowned. "So what? He used to work for Emerson. Those guys are friends of his. You're not saying that Julio had anything to do with..."

"I'm just saying what I saw."

"If you want my opinion," Ellie cut in, "you don't have to look any farther than next door to find out who's behind all this."

"Please, Ellie," said Jim.

Alec could see Ellie starting to get hot. "I can't believe you guys. Rotasky is the one who stands to gain the most if we go down. It's so obvious!"

O'Brien held up his hands. "Don't you people start

squabbling. That won't get us anywhere. You're both right in telling me whatever you think is important." The sheriff sighed and then looked at his watch. "The best thing you all can do is keep your eyes open. In the meantime, I'm going to impound this harness as evidence."

The phone rang, and Wes picked up the call. It was from the studio. The producers were sending an agent from their insurance company to the ranch to make a report. Despite the wagon accident, they had decided to go ahead with the PSA. Now more than ever, the relationship between *Drover Days* and the Humane Council needed to be straightened out. Alec listened to Wes and the man on the phone discuss the most immediate problem—finding an actor to fill in for Dousette.

Wes hung up the phone. He said that the producers wanted a "name" actor for the spot. Yet finding someone available on such short notice wouldn't be easy, even under normal circumstances.

Jim snapped his fingers. "Hey, wait a minute. We don't have to go scrounging around the casting office for some would-be cowboy star." He put his hand on Alec's shoulder. "We have one of the most famous horsemen in the country standing right here."

"Right," Alec said with a laugh. He looked at the others, who just stared back at him. No one else was laughing. The smile slowly worked its way off Alec's face.

"How about it, Alec?" asked Wes. "You could easily play Dousette's part in this thing. It's simple."

"But I'm no actor."

"You don't have to be. Just ride through the canyon

with Kramer and Doug Maxwell, the actor who plays Jed, while Frank paces you in the camera car. It'd be a cakewalk for you. The rest, voice-overs and whatnot, we could take care of in the studio later."

Alec let the idea sink in for a moment. After the fire and what happened to Pal Joey, it seemed obvious that being on the set with Wes Taylor wasn't the safest place in the world these days. Yet he liked Ellie and Wes, and his impulse was to help them out. If Kramer and Maxwell were still going through with the shoot, how could he refuse? On the other hand, Alec felt leery of getting involved with Wes Taylor and his crazy business.

"I don't know, Wes," said Alec.

"Imagine the look on Henry Dailey's face when he sees you on TV with Paul Kramer." The thought made Alec smile.

The others watched Alec and waited for him to answer. Finally he shrugged and said, "Well, that doesn't seem so bad. Sure. Why not?"

Wes gave Alec a slap on the back. "Fan-tastic. You're a lifesaver, kid."

Alec walked over to the tack room to get his saddle and bridle. As he came outside, Wes was waiting by the door. The old cowboy caught the puzzled look on Alec's face. He seemed to be reading Alec's mind. "Wondering what you're getting yourself into? Don't sweat it, Alec. This should be a cinch."

"Somehow I feel like I'm forgetting the reason I came here. It certainly wasn't to start making commercials, even if they are for a good cause."

"The Black will get over that shadow-shying business, believe me. Just keep on working him into it nice and slow, like yesterday."

"I'm going to take him out to the driveway in a little while and see if we can make any more progress."

Wes's voice softened. "I'm sorry you had to be here for this. Joey, I mean. Guess it's been a rough couple of days for you and the Black."

"Tell me about it," said Alec. He sighed and walked away.

→ CHAPTER 14 ←

Guessing Games

lec carried his saddle, pads and bridle out to the Black's corral. California sunlight brushed everything with a warm golden color. Two argumentative blue jays squawked at each other from the upper branches of a eucalyptus. Otherwise, Taylor Ranch was unusually quiet.

The Black waited for Alec at the corral gate. Alec spoke to his horse, looking up into the stallion's huge, dark eyes. Tiny reflections of his own face stared back at him. He stood there a moment, wondering how the Black really saw him. Did the Black remember Alec as the boy whose life he saved in a shipwreck so many years ago? Could either of them ever forget their struggle for survival on that deserted island? So much had changed since then, yet the bond between them remained. Alec and the Black belonged to each other.

Afternoon shadows were just beginning to fall when Alec reined the Black out of the corral. They rode down the driveway and alongside the blacktop road fronting the pasture. Inside the fence, some of the other horses nickered as the stallion went by.

Keeping to the shoulder, Alec and the Black followed the road past the entrance to Sagebrush. Luckily, there was no traffic to contend with. Alec breathed deep and easy. His thoughts wound back to the wagon accident and the question of the cut harness lines. With all the other things going wrong at the ranch recently, the accident couldn't be seen as just a single event. It must be part of a pattern.

Perhaps the person responsible was a core member of the film crew, someone who was there for almost every scene. One by one, Alec began to consider everyone he could think of, from director to production assistant. Halfway through his list, Alec stopped. Why would any of the crew want to harm *Drover Days?* It would put them out of a job. Unless they were being paid off on the side or there was some other unknown reason, that didn't make sense.

This fact was doubly true for those who lived at the ranch. Jim seemed a devoted member of the family. Mike had already proven his loyalty by trying to save the wagon team from crashing. No one at the ranch or on the crew had any known reason to hurt *Drover Days,* though they might have the most opportunities.

Then suddenly Alec thought of Julio. Why was he talking to those men from Emerson's Ranch? The question quickly answered itself: because he used to work for them. They were his friends. With a sigh, he shifted his weight in his saddle and tried not to think about it anymore.

Alec turned the Black around when he reached a gas station on the outskirts of Sky View Terrace. By the time they arrived back at the ranch gate, the afternoon shadows were fanning out around trees and buildings like dark liquid. Shadows. Before this week Alec would have hardly noticed them. Now they seemed to be everywhere.

Alec rode through the gate at the driveway entrance. Up ahead, a dark shadow hung down from the eucalyptus trees and spread out across the midpoint of the driveway. At the shadow's edge, the stallion pulled up. He began pawing the dirt, then half reared. He threw back his head and tossed his inky mane. A breeze rustled the leaves of the eucalyptus trees towering overhead. Long, dark seed pods helicoptered down from the upper branches and scattered onto the ground.

The Black flicked his ears and listened. Slight tremors rippled the stallion's coat. Beads of sweat glistened on his flanks.

Alec thought about what he had to do. He leaned forward, pressing his head next to the Black's neck. Clucking softly, he cued the Black to back up into the shadow. The response was tentative, almost awkward, but at last the Black stood quietly in the shadow, just as he had the day before.

So far, so good, Alec thought. The next step was to get the Black to cross the shadow headfirst. Moving out into sunlight again, Alec reined the Black around. The stallion brought his head within a foot of the shadow's edge and then stopped.

Alec didn't try to force the Black to move farther. He began whistling, soft and low. After a minute, he tried coaxing the Black forward with gentle rocking and the urging of leg pressure. The Black wouldn't budge. Alec started up a one-sided conversation with his horse, talking about his upcoming TV debut. "It might be fun, you know. I sort of wish we could do it together, but I can't risk having you around the set anymore, not the way things have been going lately. It's enough of a risk to take myself." He talked about Wes and Ellie and the woes of Taylor Ranch. And Alec rambled on about his own personal problems. The words themselves were unimportant. All that mattered was the flow of sound, familiar and reassuring.

The Black swished his tail at flies. He fluttered his nostrils and twitched his ears. Alec waited patiently. From time to time, he tried another gentle nudge to lure the big horse forward into the shadow. When he did, the Black resisted stubbornly, bracing himself and keeping his hooves planted firmly on the ground.

Alec dismounted to give the Black's back a rest. He stood by the Black's head, puzzling over the nature of this thing that troubled his horse. What did the stallion feel, Alec wondered. He kicked at the carpet of seed pods in frustration. "Come on, Black. They're not holes, just shadows. You won't trip." The stallion arched his neck. It made him look larger than life, proud and defiant. His eyes caught the sunlight and flashed brilliantly.

This wasn't getting them anywhere, Alec thought. He walked the Black down the drive toward the gate, then turned around and came back to the shadows again.

Alec assumed the Black would avoid the shadows as before. But this time the Black passed freely through one shadow after another. Alec pinched himself to make sure he wasn't dreaming. Not since Ruskin's accident had the stallion crossed a line of shadow on anything vaguely resembling a racetrack.

"That's it, fella. Good boy!" Hooking his foot into a stirrup, Alec swung himself into the saddle and tried to retrace the stallion's steps. But with Alec up, the stallion began to balk again. Alec tried to figure out what was going on. Could it be that the Black balked at shadows only when Alec was riding him?

For the first time, it dawned on Alec that he might be the one with the shadow phobia, not the Black. Perhaps Ruskin's spill at Santa Anna had frightened him more than he knew. Maybe he had been unconsciously telegraphing his own fear to the Black ever since. It was hard for him to accept the idea that he could have a problem this big and not know it. He reined the Black around and started back to find Wes.

Outside the office Wes stood talking with a man in a suit who Alec guessed was the insurance agent sent by the production company. After the man got into his car and left, Alec told Wes what had just happened. Wes listened and then nodded slowly. "I was thinking that you might have more to do with all this than you realized."

Alec frowned. "I don't feel like I'm riding different than usual. I just can't believe that it's me who's scared of shadows."

"That's easy enough to find out. Let's put someone else up on the Black, run them up the driveway and see if the Black balks at the shadow. If he doesn't, then we'll know the problem is coming from you."

Alec shook his head. "No one can ride the Black but me, Wes, remember?"

Wes snapped his fingers. "I forgot about that. Well then, if we can't test the Black with another rider, we'll have to test you with another horse."

After taking the Black back to his corral, Alec saddled Lowball and brought him out to the driveway. On Wes's signal he put Lowball in motion. The big Thoroughbred responded eagerly to Alec's urging, sweeping through one shadow after another at a gallop.

"So much for that theory," Alec said as he dismounted beside Wes. The old cowboy thought a moment.

"Maybe. But you might be more nervous on the Black than you would be on any other horse—so that last experiment's pretty meaningless."

Alec groaned. It was Wes's theory that was meaning-less. He felt like Wes was grasping at straws. Alec took off Lowball's tack and turned him loose in the pasture.

Every day that passed seemed to make the situation more confusing.

Late that night, Alec and Ellie met out by the Black's corral. Alec told her about the training session. "Yesterday I felt sure that the Black was recovering. Now I'm starting to question myself as well as the Black." Ellie heard the frustration in Alec's voice.

"At least the Black isn't as hung up as you thought he was."

"Yes, but we still can't race."

Ellie didn't let him feel sorry for himself very long. "You think you have problems? I've just been doing the books. A couple more weeks like this and Rotasky will be calling this Sagebrush West." She gestured around her and then looked up at the stars. "Just be glad you're not in a hospital bed, like Dousette."

"How's he making out, anyway?"

"They're keeping him under observation in case of internal injuries. If he checks out okay, they should release him in a few days."

After a moment's silence, Ellie told Alec that she'd been looking around the tack room earlier. "Thought maybe I could uncover a clue to who got in there and cut those reins. I didn't find anything, though."

"You know, accidents do just happen sometimes."

"Maybe so. But it doesn't take a genius to figure out who'll benefit if things keep fouling up and we start missing our loan payments. This land is valuable, and Rotasky wants it."

They sat there a while longer, and then Ellie said, "It's getting late. Think I'll turn in."

"Me too."

As she jumped down from the fence Ellie caught the heel of her boot on the lower rail. She slipped and fell to the ground. Alec reached out and lifted her to her feet. Still holding hands, they started back toward the house. Alec gently squeezed her fingers. She returned the gesture before letting go.

"I don't mean to pry," Alec said, "but doesn't it get lonely for you around here? Don't you have a boyfriend or anything?"

"At the moment I wouldn't know what to do with one."

"I was wondering if maybe you and Mike..."

Ellie smiled. "No. We're just friends. Mike's into his career and trying to learn what he can from Pops. Besides, I have the ranch to think about. That's plenty."

Alec nodded. "Just like I have the Black."

"And the Black has you. Right now there's no room for anything else, for either of us."

Side by side, they strolled quietly down the rest of the path. Alec said good night and set out for his trailer. As he lay in bed thinking things over, he began to feel a little angry with himself. Every day he seemed to become more involved with the ranch and further from uncovering a cure to the shadow shying. What had possessed him to sign on to do that stupid PSA? He let out a deep sigh. Whatever it was, there would be no turning back now.

✧ CHAPTER 15 ✧

More Surprises

By the time Alec finished feeding the Black the next morning, the place was swarming with cast and crew. The day's schedule called for taping a fake fight between Rex and a big stag deer. It sounded risky. Even by himself, Rex could be a handful and a half. Alec wondered how Wes was going to manage the stunt.

Inside the filming corral, the *Drover Days* crew set up the sound, camera and lighting equipment. After yesterday's accident, no one was taking any chances. They checked and rechecked the equipment down to the last detail, then checked it again. As always, they joked around while they worked. Yet there was something desperate in the air, something forced about their laughter, as if they just wanted to get the scene over with before anything else went wrong.

In the empty corral adjoining the filming corral the

wranglers were heightening the fence with extensions. It could then serve as a holding pen for the stag. Mike was back at work today, limping a bit but not complaining. Alec helped Mike nail together a wooden chute connecting the two corrals for the stag.

Alec looked up from his work when he heard voices arguing. Predictably, one of them belonged to Wes. The other was Marty Fisher's.

Marty waved his hands in the air. "Sure, I'm mad. What do you expect? You're the one who's supposed to be in charge of the animals here."

"That's right. I am the one who put Joey down. There was no other choice. And if it happened all over again tomorrow, I'd do the same thing. I won't let an animal suffer if there's no hope for him."

Marty drew a deep breath to calm his anger. "Look, Wes, this isn't the first problem we've had with you on this shoot. You've been stretching the rules since day one. Some of the people back at the office are saying we're not tough enough on trainers like you."

"Not tough enough?" Wes balled his hands into fists. "Come on! The horses on *Drover Days* get better treatment than the actors—more breaks, shorter hours, no overtime."

"What happened to Joey makes us all look bad."

"In all the years I've been working in this business, I've never lost an animal like that."

"This is the last warning, Wes. We're going strictly by the book from now on. Any more screwups and the Humane Council will have to withhold approval of the show. You know what that would mean. The networks won't touch it."

They stood in silence a moment while Wes managed to get hold of his temper. He must have realized that arguing with Marty wasn't getting him anywhere. "I'm sorry, Marty. I know I fly off the handle with people sometimes. But never with my animals. You know that."

Marty nodded. "You push them pretty hard sometimes, Wes."

"Sure, but I always get the job done without anyone getting hurt."

"Until yesterday."

"Yeah," echoed Wes, "until yesterday."

A white ragtop Cadillac pulling a small horse trailer came rumbling up the drive and parked by the shooting corral. A burly man with a shaved head and a blond goatee stepped out of the driver's seat. Three young assistants followed him.

Ignoring everyone around him, the bald man in the shiny black boots strode to the other side of the corral. Relaxed, almost catlike, he exuded confidence, as if he owned the place and was walking a few inches higher off the earth than everybody else. The man began testing the sturdiness of the extensions in the holding pen.

"Who's that?" Alec asked Mike.

"Andre, the trainer who'll be handling the stag for today's shoot." Mike smiled. "Andre used to train animals for the circus. He doesn't communicate. He dominates."

"How's he get along with Wes?"

"How do you think?"

Alec could imagine the clash of egos between the two trainers. "Not too well, I suspect."

"They've managed to work together before, barely. In this business, all the trainers have to draw from the same well."

Andre finished his inspection of the chute and extensions. With a grunt of approval, he hopped into his Caddy, backed the trailer up to the holding-pen gate and barked an order to his helpers. They opened the trailer door. A stag with an imposing rack of horns rushed out of the trailer and darted around the pen.

Alec watched the stag lower his head and shake his horns. "That stag looks fractious enough."

"You should have seen the bear Andre brought over last year. Ha! That animal wasn't tamed, much less trained. Andre's animals respect the whip and that's about it."

"Isn't it going to be dangerous bringing Rex and the stag together? What if they start fighting for real?"

Mike kept his eyes on the stag. "They won't. We've done this before. Those two are more scared of each other than anything else. We're going to have to hook them up and pull them together with cables."

"How's that?"

"See that clump of grass in the center of the corral? That's camouflaging a couple of pulleys anchored to a railroad tie we buried in the center of the corral. Our cable will run from Rex's harness through one of the pulleys. By pulling on the other end of the cable, we can stand off to the side and drag Rex into position. Andre's people will do the same—the stag will be hooked up to their cable from the opposite side."

"Won't you see the cables?"

Mike shook his head. "No. They're so fine the cameras will barely pick them up, especially when they're drawn tight. The trick is keeping the cameras at a distance and playing with the focus. If the cameraman does it right, the cables will disappear completely on screen."

Wes called his wranglers over for a quick conference. Then he sent Mike and the others to man their end of the cable at a spot along the fence halfway across the corral. Andre's assistants mirrored their actions from the other side. Two camera crews took up vantage points along the edge of the fence. It looked as if shooting was about to begin.

Wes brought Rex in from the pasture and positioned him across the corral from the stag's chute. Only after looking carefully could Alec see the harness Rex wore. It crisscrossed the Morgan's chest and had been dyed to match the color of his coat. The effect rendered it practically invisible.

Rex began acting skittish. Wes waved a lash whip high in the air off camera to get his attention and keep him focused. In the far corner, Andre had the stag in the narrow wooden chute. His arms were locked around the stag's neck. He used his massive bulk to keep the animal still. Wes ordered Julio to stand by to cut Rex's cable in case of an emergency. On their side of the corral, one of

Andre's helpers also stood ready with a pair of long-handled wire cutters.

"Tell me when you're all set!" the director shouted to Wes and Andre.

The answers came back fast. "Go ahead." "Let's do it."

Frank gave the go-ahead signal to the trainers. The fine cables were clipped onto the harnesses.

"Action!" cried the director.

Hand over hand, the cable crews began to pull their ends of the two cables. The wires drew taut.

Frank signaled the cameramen. "Roll tape!"

Rex and the stag slowly drew toward the center of the corral. Shrill whistles and grunts filled the air. The Morgan reeled back on his hind legs as the stag bounced stiffly toward him. The closer they were pulled to each other, the more they struggled against the invisible cables. Their every move was shadowed by the two camera crews.

If Alec hadn't known about the cables, he would have thought the animal performers actually were facing off to do battle. In reality, they just wanted to get away from each other. The only fighting going on was against the cables holding them.

Over and over again, the cable crews pulled Rex and the stag into position. The two animals never came closer than fifteen feet apart. It all looked terrific to Alec, but Frank wasn't satisfied. The director wanted more footage and kept retaking the scene. Every few takes the camera crew tried another shooting angle. As much time was spent adjusting the cameras and lighting between shots as on the actual filming.

Across the corral Alec could see Marty Fisher pacing back and forth, watching everything from the sidelines. Frank wanted to keep taping. Marty looked at Wes and tapped his wrist, signaling the trainer to hold up. Alec looked at his own watch. Almost an hour had passed since they started shooting.

"Break time!" Wes called out.

"What!" cried Frank.

Without saying anything, Wes looked in the direction of Marty. Frank glowered at Marty. "Come on, Marty. Just one more run-through. We're almost done."

"Sorry, Frank. You know the rules. These animals need a rest."

The crew broke up. The camera operators huddled together with Frank. Most of the others headed to the snack table for coffee. Wes and Andre unhitched the animals from their cables.

Suddenly there was the thunder of a loud motor from the direction of Sagebrush. Someone over at the development was starting up a bulldozer.

Panicked by the noise, the stag broke away from Andre. He bolted across the corral. Crewmen scattered. Someone knocked over a light stand. In one seemingly effortless leap, the stag sailed over the corral fence and disappeared into the trees. Andre cursed loudly and ran after him. His assistants joined in the chase.

In the confusion, Rex pulled free of Wes. Like the stag, he charged the fence and cleared the top rail. Only Rex didn't run off. Once outside the fence, the big Morgan shrilled with rage. He turned his fury on the first person he could find, Marty Fisher.

"Whoa!" Marty shouted. Rex didn't respond except to flatten his ears and show his teeth. The Morgan plunged past Marty like a charging bull. He slid to a stop and whirled to face Marty again. The humane man could do nothing but stand his ground. He was in a fix and knew it. "Taylor!" he cried. "Get this animal of yours away from me."

Wes, Mike and the other wranglers jogged over. "Hang on, Mr. Fisher!" Julio shouted. Rex moved in on Marty again, slowly this time. He must have read the fear in Marty's eyes. The oversized Morgan was toying with the humane man, almost like a cat playing with a trapped mouse. Rex edged closer, backing Marty up against a tree.

"Easy, boy. Easy now," Marty stammered. Rex snorted and stamped his hooves. Before he could charge again, Marty scrambled up the trunk of the tree. Rex began circling the tree trunk as Marty clung desperately to the lower branches.

When the wranglers finally arrived, Mike managed to get a lead line on Rex. Wes called up to Marty. "How'd you get Rex so riled up, Marty? I guess no one told him who you are."

"Very funny, Taylor."

"Come on down, now. We have work to do. We can't spend all day climbing around in trees like you."

"Easy now, Rex. Atta boy," Mike soothed the Morgan as he led him away.

Wes turned and looked up at the treed humane man. "Coast is clear, Marty."

Marty unglued himself from the tree and slid down to the ground, landing with a thump and a groan. Dusting himself off, the humane man turned his anger on Wes. "What have you done to that poor creature, anyway?"

"Done to him?"

"He's vicious. A perfect example of what happens to an abused animal."

Wes laughed. "That's just his nature, Marty. Rex has been about as well treated as anyone could ask for. I know the man who bred him."

Marty kept up his tirade about abused animals, but some of the righteousness left his voice. Alec thought he sounded like his pride was hurt more than anything.

Frank came up behind Wes, his temper seething. "Every day, Taylor! Every day something goes wrong with these animals of yours."

"Me! Talk to Andre about that crazy buck of his. Talk to the idiot who cranked up that dozer when we were still working." Nose to nose, hands on their hips, Wes and Frank went at each other like an umpire and an outraged manager.

When Ellie appeared, Wes broke off his argument with Frank and shifted his anger to her. "Ellie! What's the matter with you! Didn't you give Rotasky our shooting schedule for this morning? I thought we had an agreement with those people!"

Ellie's voice was calm and clear. "We do. I sent our schedule over last week. He promised me they wouldn't use any heavy machinery while we were shooting at the ranch."

"You did, huh? So what happened?"

"Don't ask me. Jim went over to talk with the driver just now. Maybe Rotasky figures all bets are off, since you pulled that gun on him the other day."

Wes grumbled something and turned back to argue with Frank some more. The director threw his cap to the ground and started pulling at his hair. His voice rose. "I don't care. I don't care. *I don't care*! I've wasted too much time already. Set up for the next shot. We'll shoot without sound if we have to."

The wranglers brought the horses in from their pasture for the next scene. Just as things seemed to be calming down, Jim came running toward them shouting, "Wes! Wes! You've gotta come quick!"

"Settle down, Jim."

"It's Sagebrush! That dozer of theirs just crossed our property line. They knocked over Sinbad's grave marker and..."

"What the...! Didn't the fool driver see the fence?"

"He ran right over it. Said he was just following the markers left by the survey team."

Frank looked up to heaven in a plea for help. "Great. Another crisis. Why would I expect anything else?"

Wes ignored him and looked around for Mike. "Mike! Get over here!" Mike left the horses with Patrick and Julio and came hobbling up. Wes handed Mike his lash whip. "Think you can take over for me here?"

"Sure, boss. No problem. Don't worry about a thing."

Wes turned to Frank. "I'll be right back, Frank. Mike can work the horses in the next scene. He knows what to do."

Before Frank could answer, Wes hustled off to his truck. Mike smiled, as if glad to have a chance to prove himself on his own. Alec and Ellie looked at each other a moment and then ran after Wes.

→ CHAPTER 16 ←

Risky Business

As Wes opened the truck door, Ellie slid onto the passenger seat from the other side. Alec jumped in beside her. Wes's face twisted angrily, but his voice only sounded weary. "Where do you two think you're going?"

Ellie shrugged innocently. "I want to hear Rotasky explain this. Anyway, we have to keep an eye on you."

"Okay, but just listen. No mouthing off."

Rotasky's office, actually one wing of a model home, was in a peaceful corner of Sagebrush Village. A row of tall oaks stood shoulder to shoulder at one end of the lawn; a flock of doves bustled around the piles of dead leaves raked neatly under the trees.

Rotasky's overgrown driver answered the doorbell with a snarl. "Yeah?"

"Where's the boss?"

"Not here." Wes leaned in and tried to look around the doorman, who blocked the entrance with his body. Wes tried to push past.

"That's okay, Bobby," called a voice from inside. "Let Mr. Taylor and his granddaughter in."

Alec hesitated. "Maybe I'll just wait out here." Ellie tugged on Alec's arm and pulled him along.

Rotasky sat at his desk in one corner of a sparsely furnished room. The synthetic smell of new carpet hung in the air. A scale model of Sagebrush was displayed prominently inside a glass case set on a table in the middle of the floor.

Rotasky flashed an insincere smile. "Something we can do for you, Mr. Taylor?" The driver moved behind Rotasky and stared at them menacingly.

Wes got right to the point. "I thought you agreed to have your bulldozers work around our shooting schedule."

"That's true. I believe…well, let's just see." Opening a drawer, the little man consulted a sheet of paper. "According to the schedule you gave us, you weren't supposed to be shooting at the ranch today."

Wes looked at Ellie accusingly. "Didn't you tell him we pushed everything back a day after the fire?"

Ellie's cheeks colored red with embarrassment. "Sorry, Pops. I guess I forgot."

Rotasky cleared his throat to get their attention. "Now, if there's nothing else…"

"As a matter of fact, there is one little thing," said Wes.

"What's the big idea of sending your bulldozer *onto my land?*"

"Your land? What are you talking about?"

"That dozer has been pushing up against the property line for days. Just now it crossed over, ran down our fence and a grave marker."

Rotasky returned Wes's accusations with a look of surprise. The bodyguard shifted his legs as Wes stepped closer and leaned over the desk.

Wes's voice hardened. "We have a situation here, Rotasky. I want to know what you're going to do about it."

Rotasky straightened his shoulders and sat back. His voice became formal and lawyerly. "Any incursions upon your property were entirely accidental, I can assure you."

Ellie couldn't keep quiet any longer. "Accidental, huh? Just like the generator fire and the wagon crash? Come on, Rotasky. We know you're behind what's been going on at the ranch."

Wes stepped in front of her. "Be quiet, Ellie."

Rotasky's mouth hung open as he tried to digest what Ellie had said. Then he shook his head with faint bewilderment. Muttering under his breath, he looked at his watch pointedly. "Someone obviously moved the survey markers around the area where the bulldozer was working. Vandals, probably. As for these accusations..." Rotasky glanced at his bodyguard. "Bobby, will you please escort Ms. Taylor and her friend outside? Mr. Taylor and I would like to speak privately for a moment." Bobby moved toward them slightly.

Wes eyed Rotasky warily and then turned to Ellie and Alec. "It's okay. Go ahead. I'll be out in a minute." Alec took Ellie by the arm and walked her to the door. Bobby followed to make sure they didn't get lost on the way.

Five minutes later Wes came outside again and waved Alec and Ellie back to the truck. Ellie waited for Wes to say something. He didn't speak until they had turned out onto the canyon road. "What do you think you're doing, accusing Rotasky like that?"

"Why are you defending him now?"

Wes sighed as he turned onto the ranch driveway. "Rotasky's our neighbor. We have to live together."

"Oh, really? You're the one who pulled the shotgun on the guy."

"That was a stupid thing to do and we both know it."

"So what's the story, Pops?"

"The story is, we came to an agreement."

"I thought so."

"If we forget about the fence and grave marker, Rotasky has promised to forget his complaints about us."

"That's all?"

"What do you want, blood?"

"I don't know how Rotasky's doing it, but—"

Wes cut her short. "Two words, Ellie. Prove it. No matter what you think, there just isn't any hard evidence linking Rotasky with the accidents on *Drover Days*." Ellie fumed angrily but didn't speak. She must have known Wes was right.

Wes pulled the truck to a stop and went to see if Mike was having any problems with the horses. Alec walked

Ellie back to the office. "Well, what do you think now?" she asked him.

"I really don't know, Ellie."

"Rotasky must be paying off someone on the crew. He just has to be."

"Like who?"

"I've been thinking some more about Julio. All this trouble started just around the time he signed on here." Even as she said this, she didn't sound very sure of herself.

Alec shrugged. "You know him better than I do."

"I still say Rotasky knows more than he's saying."

Alec shook his head. "Last night I might have agreed with you."

"Last night? What about today?"

"Now I'm not so sure. I'm no mind reader, but Rotasky looked genuinely surprised when you accused him."

"So what was Rotasky up to with that bulldozer?"

"Whatever it is, I don't think he's directing some conspiracy against the ranch or *Drover Days*. What happened was probably a mistake, like he said."

"That's it?"

"That's it, Ellie. Running over a fence with a bulldozer isn't sabotage. The people we want would never go in for such a blatant attack. That's not how they operate."

Alec spent the next hour feeding and grooming the Black. He enjoyed the familiar routine almost as much as the Black did. When he finally put away the rub rag, the stallion's coat shone like new velvet.

After lunch, the crew went back to work filming another scene for *Drover Days*. Alec had seen enough TV work for one day. He took the Black out for a ride, passing Sagebrush and continuing on the road toward town. By the time he returned to Taylor's, afternoon shadows were streaking the driveway. Alec brought the Black to the edge of the shadow. As he had yesterday, the stallion refused to cross the line between dark and light with Alec in the saddle.

Alec saw Wes walking toward him. The old trainer waved him over. "Henry called when you were out. He said he found tickets home for you and the Black on Friday."

"Great."

"Any luck with your horse?"

"It's the same deal. By himself, he doesn't seem to mind the shadows much at all anymore. With me up, though, he's worse than ever."

Wes scratched his head, as if he were holding back from speaking his mind. "Be patient, Alec. Sometimes this sort of problem will take care of itself. You never know."

Alec listened quietly to Wes's generalized optimism. This positive-attitude stuff could be a bit overbearing at times, Alec thought. He wasn't a child. He knew very well that things didn't always work out the way you wanted, no matter how you tried. Why couldn't the old cowboy just admit that he was stumped and didn't have the faintest idea how to help the Black overcome the shadow shying? Certainly he wasn't still holding on to the idea that this was mainly Alec's problem?

"What about the PSA tomorrow?" asked Alec. "I'm still not sure what I'm supposed to do."

Wes grinned. "It'll be a snap, Alec. I told you that before. Boy, you shoulda heard the producer when I told him that I got you and the Black for the PSA. He couldn't believe it."

Alec nearly dropped the reins. "The Black! You didn't say anything about wanting to use the Black in this thing."

"Well, I just naturally figured you'd want to ride him."

"The Black's a whole different deal, Wes, especially after what's been happening around here lately. I thought you were going to put me up on one of your horses."

"But now the producer is expecting you and the Black together." Wes looked startled. He sounded as surprised as Alec by the misunderstanding. "Come on, Alec," pleaded Wes. "The press releases have already been sent. You can't back out on us."

Alec couldn't believe this. What had he gotten himself into? He dismounted, shaking his head. "I can't risk it, Wes. You saw those cut reins. Something strange is going on around here, and I don't want the Black to get mixed up in it. Besides, you know the Black isn't himself right now."

"There aren't any shadows to worry about where we'll be going. And I doubt you'll even have to break the Black out of a slow trot. Just go for a ride with the others and forget about the camera."

"But Wes..."

"You won't be alone up there. I'll be with you the whole time." Wes waited for Alec to say something, then looked him straight in the eye. "I'd never let anything happen to the Black. Believe me."

"Just like Pal Joey, huh?" Wes turned away. When he looked back, Alec could see the hurt showing in the old cowboy's face. "I'm sorry, Wes," said Alec, "but this seems to have turned into a very risky business right now."

Wes's voice softened. "Please, Alec. Don't make me beg. We've really put ourselves on the line this time. Please." He took a deep breath to collect himself. "Just give it a try with the Black. If he starts acting up or if you see anything you don't like, we'll pull him out and put you up on another horse. You have my word."

Mixed emotions tugged at Alec's heart. It was true that he and the Black took risks all the time. But taking risks with the Black on the racetrack was one thing; taking them for this silly PSA seemed crazy. On the other hand, Kramer and Maxwell didn't seem to be frightened. And Wes's proposal sounded fair enough. If Wes really meant what he said, maybe it would be all right.

Alec slowly nodded. "Okay, Wes. I'll try it. But I'm holding you to your word. If I see anything, and I mean anything..."

Wes's face brightened. "You got it, Alec. When it comes to the Black, whatever you say goes."

"Okay, then."

"Great. You'll see; it'll be easy. Even Frank should be

obliging at this point. I'd wager that right now he wants to get this thing over with as much as we do."

By that night Alec had become a little more at ease with the idea of riding the Black in the PSA. He'd make sure the Black was safe. He'd keep his eyes open. At the first sign of trouble the Black would be out of there. And everyone else was sure to be on guard also. Wes, Frank, Kramer, Maxwell: they were all professionals. Surely they wouldn't take any unnecessary risks.

Jim sat on the porch, listening to the radio. He roped Alec into playing a few hands of gin.

"Getting anywhere with the Black?" asked Jim.

"Nowhere," said Alec. "I hate to say it, but it looks like this whole trip is turning out to be a bust as far as the Black and I are concerned."

"At least you tried. And if Wes can't help the Black, I don't know who can."

"Where's Mike tonight?" Alec asked.

"Who knows? Probably went into town. I wonder what's bothering him. He's been acting a mite cranky all afternoon."

"Maybe his leg is hurting him."

"I think he's still brooding over what happened to Joey. Or who knows, could be he's in love. You never can tell what's up with that guy."

Even though they'd spent a good bit of time together, Alec felt he knew Mike the least of all the people at Taylor Ranch. The young wrangler was a horseman like Alec and the closest to him in age. Yet those similarities hadn't brought them together as they might have.

Jim dealt the cards. "Mike reminds me of myself when I was a young hotshot buckaroo. He's better at handling horses than I ever was, though. That boy has God-given talent. He could go off on his own right now and make a living for himself if he wanted to."

"Think so?"

"You bet. If it wasn't for Wes, Mike would have packed his bags a long time ago. Mike wants to learn about stunt riding and handling picture horses. And there isn't another trainer working in Hollywood who can match Wes's know-how when it comes to that."

"I imagine Wes can be a pretty tough teacher, though."

"Sure. But Mike would rather be kicked by Wes than knighted by the queen of England."

Jim dealt out a few hands of gin, winning each time. Finally Alec called it quits. He said good night and walked over to his trailer.

Only one more day and his visit to Taylor Ranch would be over, Alec thought. He'd be glad to get home. Maybe Henry could come up with some new plan to help the Black. One way or the other, it looked like they were all right back where they started.

→CHAPTER 17←

Barrel Rider

Will you hold still, Black." Alec groaned as he tried to move around his horse without being kicked or stomped. The Black was acting frisky this morning. He whisked his tail back and forth, then twisted his neck and reached around to nip at the brush in Alec's hand. "Come on, fella. You want to look pretty for the cameras, don't you?"

Small puffs of dust rose from the stallion's coat and melted away in streaks of sunlight as Alec worked. Soon the Black's coat shone like well-oiled leather. From beyond the trees Alec could hear the sounds of cars and trucks rumbling up the ranch driveway. He looked at his watch and saw that it was almost time to go. His instructions were to meet Frank and Wes at the tack room by seven thirty.

Halfway along the path, Alec met Ellie coming the

other way. "I was just on my way to get you," she said. "You ready?"

"As ready as I'll ever be. The Black missed you last night, by the way. Me too."

"I had to work."

Alec nodded. "Any word about Dousette?"

"He's still in the hospital. They're doing more tests. The doctor said he'll be able to leave in a day or so."

"That's good news."

"Yeah, but it's looking like he'll have to be written out of the next couple episodes of *Drover Days*, at least."

"You working in the office today?"

"Where else? Why?"

"I'd appreciate having some familiar faces around."

"Don't worry—Pops and Mike will be there."

They turned onto the corridor, passing a line of parked trucks and trailers. Wes came out of the house and called them over. "There you two are. Ellie, show Alec to the wardrobe trailer, will you?"

"I know where it is," Alec said. "But don't we have to rehearse or something? I'm still not sure what I'm supposed to do."

"We'll block it out when we get to the location. For now, go on and get yourself outfitted."

Alec walked over to the trailer. He was surprised to feel a few nervous butterflies flutter around in his stomach. Could they be the beginnings of stage fright? The thought of being on a set wasn't quite so new to him as when he'd first arrived. Only this time he'd be in front of the camera, not behind it.

Myron, the makeup man, greeted him at the door to the wardrobe trailer. In his early thirties, he was tall and bearded and dressed in a flashy shirt that looked more like a painting than something to wear. Angie, an intense, pint-size woman with a pug nose, handled the wardrobe. She tried to make Alec feel at ease as she took his measurements.

Rows of cowboy boots were lined up beneath clothes racks running the length of the trailer. Like the boots, the shirts, pants and jackets were in all sizes and conditions. Angie pulled out a particularly flashy outfit, the kind a cowboy might wear in a parade. "How'd you like to wear this today?" Alec cringed at the thought.

"Don't worry. You couldn't use this stuff anyway," said Angie with a grin. "It's Kramer's. No one else can wear it. It's in his contract. Kramer always has to be the dude, even when he's playing the part of a broncobuster."

Angie turned Alec over to Myron, who began to pat down Alec's face with powder. Alec felt trapped. Myron told him to be still. "That Black of yours is lucky to have such a lovely mane. For closeups like these, Frank usually wants to weave in extensions." Right, Alec thought. A fake mane. He could just see this guy trying to get close to the Black. Myron babbled on, "...makes it longer and more luxurious, know what I mean?"

Alec spent the next half-hour trying on different outfits. When he stepped out of the wardrobe trailer again, he wore what Angie called the "classic look": cowboy boots, jeans, a denim jacket, a red flannel shirt and a tan cowboy hat.

A production assistant met Alec by the trailer door and told him they were going to have to delay the PSA about an hour or so. Alec grabbed a cup of coffee at the snack table and walked over to the corral. It was crowded with the tools of TV production. He recognized some of the technicians from yesterday and the day before. Frank stood off to one side holding a battery-powered megaphone.

In the middle of the corral three men fiddled with an odd-looking contraption, a saddle strapped to a fifty-gallon oil drum. The drum was suspended on cables between four posts. Four ropes ran beneath it. The ropes crossed through rings welded to the bottom of the barrel and stretched out on either side.

Alec saw Ellie and Mike leaning against the corral's fence rail. He walked over to join them. "Hey. What's up?"

Ellie gave him a nod. "Kramer's going to ride the barrel. After his spill the other day we thought he'd want to postpone that scene."

"Barrel?"

"In the story he's supposed to be riding a bucking bronco."

"And he's going to ride that thing instead?"

"It's just for closeups," Ellie explained. "On-screen, no one will be able to tell the difference."

"You mean the rodeo scenes on *Drover Days* are faked?"

"Controlled is more like it. This way the cameraman can zoom in on Kramer's face without worrying about being trampled. The shots will be edited together with scenes of a stunt double riding a real bronco. Hardly any actors do their own rodeo stunts."

Mike spat out his toothpick. "Yeah, only real tough New York cowboys like Kramer can ride a barrel." His voice dripped sarcasm and disdain. "Kramer spends more time on that barrel than on his horse." Mike limped off, clearly disgusted by such silliness. Alec chuckled. Henry would be surprised to learn the facts about Paul Kramer, doughnut-wrangling King of the Wild Barrels!

Ellie nodded toward the barrel. "Want to give it a try, Alec?"

Alec swallowed his smile. "Ah, no thanks."

"Don't pay attention to Mister Macho, Alec. Riding a barrel isn't as easy as it sounds, once those guys start working the lines. You'll see." She turned to go back to the office.

Soon Alec understood what Ellie meant. A stand-in for Kramer slung himself into the saddle while the rope handlers tested the pitch and roll of the barrel. There were four handlers, two on either side. They manipulated the barrel with a rope held in each hand. Two ropes controlled the twisting motion, the other two pitched the barrel up and down. The stand-in was thrown about like someone being jerked around on a ride at an amusement park.

When Frank felt satisfied with the position of the lights, he called out, "You ready, Paul?"

Kramer walked onto the set wearing one of his trademark white leather suits. "Are you joking? Let's get this thing over with, already. I'm sick and tired of trudging out to this dump of a ranch every other day."

"Places, everyone," the director called out. The stand-in left the set. Kramer mounted the barrel and took up the reins in one hand, holding the other hand above his head. "Makeup!" yelled Frank. Myron ran over to spray bottled water on Kramer's face. The cowboy star focused his eyes on a spot to one side of the camera.

"Roll tape. Action!" shouted Frank. The rope handlers went to work. The mechanical bucking bronco began twisting from side to side and jerking up and down. Kramer's hat flew off his head as he expertly contorted his body with the undulations of the barrel.

Frank shot the scene four times before he was satisfied. Kramer began to look queasy from all the bouncing around. In between the last two takes, assistants helped him down from the saddle and over to his chair.

"What a he-man," someone snickered.

"I don't know how he does it," said someone else.

Frank leveled an icy stare over the crew. "Cut the chatter, people." If he heard the bad jokes and snide comments, they didn't seem to rile Kramer too much. Perhaps he was immune to them after all his years in the business.

Alec felt a tap on his shoulder. It was Wes. "Let's go, Alec. We're gonna be heading up the canyon soon."

→CHAPTER 18←

The PSA

A lec brought the Black in from his corral and over to the tack room. Wes showed Alec the saddle that had been picked out for the Black to wear in the PSA. It was a simple Western saddle, nowhere near as flashy as the parade saddle Kramer liked to use. Kramer's saddle was made of heavy black leather and decorated with embossed designs.

While Alec tacked up his horse, the camera car and Jeeps started out for the upper canyon. Cast and crew for the PSA were jammed inside them. Marty Fisher trailed them in his pickup, followed by Wes in his truck. Alec and the wranglers came last. As the riders turned onto the driveway, Ellie stepped out of the office door. She waved and called, "Good luck, Alec."

An hour later everyone had regrouped at a spot in the box canyon. Kramer was there, and Doug Maxwell, the actor who played Jed. Seeing the two actors together, Alec noticed how similar they looked. Maxwell could have been a younger version of Kramer—his face had the same good looks and fine bone structure. And despite his youth, Maxwell was already a famous TV personality.

Marty Fisher walked by and nodded to Alec. Now that the Black was going to be involved, it made Alec glad to see Marty there. Under the present circumstances, the more watchful eyes there were on the Black, the better Alec felt.

The Black whinnied softly as Alec dismounted. Alec's stomach churned nervously again. There had been one too many accidents the last few days for him to feel relaxed. He stroked the Black's neck gently to soothe them both.

Frank called Alec and the two actors together. Maxwell, like Alec, wore denim and flannel. Kramer still wore his white leathers.

Kramer put his arm around Alec's shoulders. "We all appreciate what you're doing, son, especially after what happened to Louie."

Alec smiled. "Wes has been helping me with the Black. I want to return the favor."

"It's all for a good cause."

"I'm still a little nervous," Alec confessed.

The old pro gave Alec a friendly squeeze and said, "You'll be fine. These PSAs are easy. Anyway, we're glad you could jump in on such short notice."

Maxwell shook Alec's hand. "I saw you at lunch and

on location the other day, but I don't think we've met formally. I'm Doug Maxwell."

"Alec Ramsay."

Maxwell gave Alec a thousand-dollar smile. "It's going to be a thrill to work with you and the Black."

"The feeling is mutual," said Alec. "We don't get a chance to meet many television stars where I come from, much less work with them."

Myron scurried around the actors and their horses. He wanted to give the Black a quick grooming. Alec shook his head. After the way things had been going on *Drover Days*, no one was getting near the Black today except him.

The makeup man turned to Frank. "His mane really could use a little spray to bring out the highlights."

Again Alec shook his head. The Black fluttered his nostrils. Frank waved Myron off. "Forget it," he said.

Myron shrugged. "If you say so."

"The Black looks fine," the director continued. "As for you, Ramsay… Give him a touch-up, will you Myron?"

"Sure, Frank."

Alec winced. "Is that really necessary?"

Myron nodded and went to work. "You must have smudged your makeup on the ride here," he said. "You don't want to have to retake a scene because of smudges or because you look too shiny or green, do you?"

"Okay, okay." Alec closed his eyes, submitting to Myron's powder pad and admonishments to stand still.

When Myron finished, Frank told the actors to mount

their horses. Kramer was astride the big Thoroughbred, Lowball. Maxwell rode a golden-colored palomino. Both horses were perfectly groomed. Not a hair was out of place.

The Black threw his head and paced in step a moment. Perhaps the closeness of the other horses, the crew and their equipment was making him a little edgy. Or maybe he could sense some of Alec's own nervousness. With a little coaxing, Alec managed to hold the Black still.

"All right, guys," Frank said. "The story goes like this: You're supposed to be wranglers on your way to round up some wild mustangs. Don't worry about the soundtrack. We'll lay it in later. The voice-over will be telling about the Adopt-a-Mustang program. Got it?" The three riders nodded in unison.

"Now for the layout. See Mike over there?" Frank pointed to a spot half a mile across the flat, where Mike sat on his horse watching them. "Think of him as a marker. I want to see you all loping along, riding straight toward him. I'll drive alongside and track you in the camera car. And don't forget, when I give the signal, turn to the camera and give me a wave. Got it?"

Alec and the actors again nodded. If this was all there was to it, Alec thought, shooting the PSA should be as simple as everyone said it would be.

The director climbed into the camera car. He kept glancing back and forth between Alec and Kramer. Just when they were about to start the scene, Frank stopped everything. "Wait a minute. Something is wrong here."

The director stepped out of the car and walked over to

where Alec and the actors waited on their horses. Frank snapped his fingers. "Hey. I know what's bugging me. Ramsay. That saddle of yours. The color is all wrong. Hmm." He pointed to Alec and Kramer. "I've got an idea. Let's try switching saddles between you two."

Alec smiled. Hadn't Wes warned him about directors pulling surprise changes at the last minute? And Alec remembered how Frank wouldn't start the wagon scene the other day before mauling Dousette's new hat.

"No way, Frank," protested Kramer. "I always get the parade saddle. It's in my contract."

"Not this time, Paul. That stipulation is about what you wear, not your horse."

"But you know this is my favorite saddle."

Frank's voice softened. "Come on, Paul. Do it for me, will you? Just this once. I'm trying to make the shot work. Think about it—a big black saddle on a big black horse. It'll look great."

Kramer's face twisted with indignation. He was about to say something but then drew a breath and changed his mind. He slipped to the ground. "Okay, Frank. Some things aren't worth arguing about. You're the boss."

Frank gave a sigh of relief. "Nice that someone around here remembers that." For his part, Alec didn't see any reason to refuse the director's request. The Black could handle the heavier saddle easily.

Alec dismounted and exchanged Kramer's black parade saddle and blanket for his own. Everything seemed in order. Just to make sure, he checked the girth strap and stirrups' stitching for any sign of wear or tampering. Satisfied, he swung himself up onto the Black's back. Wes helped Kramer with his saddle and gave the actor a boost up.

Frank looked them over and gave a satisfied smile. "There. That's the ticket." He hopped back into the camera car. "Okay, you guys. Let's go. And try to look like you're having a good time. Action! Roll tape!"

The riders started across the floor of the box canyon. Kramer rode in the middle, with Alec on the left and Maxwell on the right. The camera car drove alongside, tracking them from twenty feet away. In the distance, painted cliffs and jutting outcroppings of rock colored the background.

Frank yelled instructions to them as they went along. "Okay. We have you in focus. I'm going to start the countdown. When I say go, bump up the speed a notch. Three—two—one—go!"

On Frank's signal, Alec and the others began loping their horses. Alec pushed his weight forward. The Black's movements began to stiffen, but Alec chalked that up to the unfamiliar saddle.

Suddenly the Black jerked his head down savagely. The movement caught Alec by surprise. The reins slipped through his hands. Alec threw himself forward trying to grab them just as the stallion rose up on his hind legs and pawed the air.

The Black's ears flattened and his head swung defiantly from side to side. Hatred flashed in his dark eyes. Maxwell and Kramer frantically pulled their horses out of the way. The cries of men and horses filled the air.

"What the…"

"Look at that!"

"Incredible!"

"Help!"

The gigantic figure of the black stallion towered over everyone else. The crew in the camera car didn't know what to do. "Quick, you idiots!" Frank screamed. "Get a camera on him!"

Alec dug his heels into the stallion's back and fought with every ounce of his strength to bring the stallion down. Still the Black remained suspended in midair, teetering on his hind legs and threatening to fall over backward.

"Get out of the way!" someone screamed. The car swerved sharply to the right. Alec heaved forward again and finally the Black's forefeet came crashing to the ground. The Black plunged ahead, shrilling wildly and then clenching down on the bit in his mouth with bared teeth. Alec's heart raced and his body shook. Without reins to hold, he could only knot his fingers in the stallion's mane and try to hang on.

⇾ CHAPTER 19 ⇽

The Buzzer

Everything blurred around him in a rush of blue sky and snatches of earth. The Black's hoofbeats came in uneven spurts. As soon as Alec shifted his weight in one direction, the stallion lunged the other way. Each time the movement jerked Alec out of his seat and threw him completely off balance.

The problem wasn't just that Alec couldn't reach the reins. Nor was it the clumsy, unfamiliar saddle, or that he'd been caught unprepared by the stallion's charge. Something completely inexplicable had taken possession of the Black. All Alec could do was hang on.

He forced his mind to focus. Whatever had come over the Black, Alec could ride, with reins or without. Riding was what he did for a living. So do it, he ordered himself. It was his only hope of staying in the saddle.

The Black angled away from Mike and the scene's

intended direction. Across the canyon, Alec saw the stand of trees rise up before him. The stallion was drawn to it like a magnet. If the Black didn't change course, what happened two days before could repeat itself. Only this time it wouldn't be the wagon team running out of control and smashing into the trees, it would be Alec and the Black.

The stallion raced across the canyon like a low-flying airplane looking for a place to land. Alec swallowed. This could be it, he thought. The end. The last ride. Somehow he had to get control over the Black.

A horse and rider cut across the canyon floor toward him. Mike leaned in from his saddle and tried to grab hold of the Black's bridle. "Hang on, Alec!" the wrangler cried over the thunder of the Black's pounding hooves. "I'll stop him!"

Mike was just trying to help, but his cries only upset the Black more. Alec couldn't wave Mike off without risking a fall.

In front of them the distance to the trees was shrinking every second. Less than fifty yards away, morning shadows mired the ground. Alec forgot about Mike. The American Cup race flashed through his mind. He remembered the drive to the wire beside Ruskin. The scream of the wind in his ears became the roar of the spectators in the crowded stands. But this was no memory. This was real! Some twist of fate was forcing him to relive the stretch run at Santa Anna here in the very spot where the wagon scene had ended in disaster only two days before.

With Mike's pinto running along on one side and the stand of trees coming up fast on the other, the Black found himself hemmed in with only one way to go. Even if he'd wanted to there was no room to break away or even stop. To avoid the trees, the Black had to carry Alec straight ahead through the line of shadows. It was something he hadn't been able to do without jumping since Ruskin's spill at the American Cup.

Going this fast, Alec knew, a jump would be fatal. No horse could gather his feet beneath him again and land safely at this speed, not even the Black. He'd take a bad step coming down and that would be it.

Alec clenched his jaw. He caught himself bracing for death. To freeze up now would be disastrous. Yet he recognized the fear that suddenly took hold of him.

His mind whirled. This couldn't be happening. Not to him. Not to the Black. He wouldn't let it. Instinct drew him into focus. Ride, he told himself. Don't think, just ride. He projected himself fifty feet ahead, to the other side of the shadows. The grip of fear loosened. Rocking forward in the saddle, Alec found the strength to relax.

Blackness enveloped horse and rider. Alec let his mind go blank. The pounding of hoofbeats roared in his ears.

Trees swept by, then light burst on them again. Earth and sky jangled around him. It was over. The Black had driven straight through the pool of shadow and safely out the other side. They'd done it! Somehow, some way, they'd done it!

Before Alec could begin to appreciate what had happened, Mike's fingertips touched the Black's bridle. The stallion jerked his head as Mike took hold. Instead of being able to stop the Black, Mike was pulled off balance. He tumbled through the air and disappeared below.

The Black ran on a short way across the canyon floor, then pulled up suddenly. With a shudder, he flung his bulk to the ground. Alec dove off. The Black twisted over onto his back, rolling and writhing in the dirt as if he were trying to smash some irritating insect.

When the stallion stood up again, clouds of dust swirled around him. His head hung down, and his sweat-drenched coat was caked with dirt. The fancy saddle hung loosely beneath his belly, upside down.

Alec lay still until the world stopped spinning. As his mind cleared he could think of only one thing. He and the Black had safely crossed the line of shadow together. For the moment, how it happened or the reason why didn't matter. A broad grin stretched across his face.

Alec pulled himself slowly to his feet. His arms, back and ribs felt twisted and sore, yet nothing seemed to be broken. He wobbled shakily over to where the Black stood.

The reality of the situation slowly began to sink in. For the first time since the Black had pulled the reins from his hands, Alec had a second to think. What had happened to the Black? Why had he run off like that?

Alec came to the stallion's side and reached back to unfasten the girth strap. The Black shuddered, taking thundering breaths. "Everything's all right now, fella," Alec soothed. "We did it." The hanging saddle and blanket dropped to the ground. The Black shoved Alec aside and stomped the saddle with his hooves.

"Easy, fella. Easy, now," Alec said, and then joined the Black in giving the fancy saddle a swift kick. "Piece of junk," he muttered to himself. Pushing closer to the Black, Alec lightly ran his hands over the big, muscled frame. Good, he thought. There was no sign of injury. The Black shook Alec off again. Alec stepped back and let him alone.

Both he and the Black had been lucky. But what about Mike? He looked back toward the trees. Patrick and Julio were dismounting. They hurried over to Mike's prone figure and knelt down beside him.

An ex–rodeo rider like Mike must be used to taking hard falls, Alec guessed. Yet this time he wasn't getting up after his spill. Wes's Jeep careened to a stop by the trees, followed by the camera car and more Jeeps. Production assistants pulled a reflector board from the back of one of the Jeeps. They crowded together and, using the board like a stretcher, lifted Mike onto it.

Wes left the others to see about Alec and the Black. "What in the name of blazes happened back there?" he cried. "That crazy horse of yours went berserk."

"Did you see us cut through that shadow? The Black didn't even flinch! Eee-ha!"

Wes shook his head. "That was some riding, kid."

Alec dusted off his pants. When he picked up the saddle and blanket from the ground, the Black shied away from him. "It's okay, fella. Nothing's going to hurt you." The Black drew back again, tossing his head and snorting. Alec kept his words flowing and tried to calm his horse.

Folding the blanket, Alec felt something unusual in the fabric, a small lump taped along the edge. He hadn't noticed it when he'd switched saddles and blankets with Kramer. The black tape blended perfectly with the color of the blanket, camouflaging the lump completely.

"Is that what was bothering you?" Alec asked, fingering the tape. Something pricked his fingers and an electric shock jolted him. He dropped the blanket to the dirt and cried, "Ouch! What the…"

Wes picked up the blanket. He touched the lump, then jerked his hand away. Pulling out his knife, he carefully slit the tape. Something fell out: a small battery pack with two tiny wires bent down from one end.

It was a "buzzer," a homemade device that corrupt jockeys sometimes used on their mounts. Alec had never actually seen a buzzer before. He'd only heard Henry and some of the older trainers talking about them. It delivered a jolt of electricity as strong as the shock from an exposed light socket and was intended to make a horse run faster. A jockey could palm a buzzer in his hand, use it at the start of the race, then toss it away along the backstretch. Being caught with a buzzer at the track could get you barred from racing for life.

So this was why the Black went berserk, Alec thought. Wes poked at the thing and picked it up. There was a button on one side. He looked at Alec. "You know what this is, don't you?"

Alec frowned. "Yeah. That button must turn on the juice."

Wes nodded slowly. "I read a story in the paper last

year about a jockey down at Del Mar being caught with one of these gizmos. Some boneheaded stuntmen used to use them in the old days, too."

"Really?"

"That was a long time ago. The folks at the Humane Council would have a fit if they thought we'd put that thing there intentionally."

Alec took a closer look at the buzzer. "If that button turns it on, I wonder why it didn't go off earlier when Kramer was riding with this saddle blanket. He weighs a lot more than I do."

Wes took the buzzer from Alec and dropped it into his shirt pocket. He pulled at his mustache and thought a moment. "Maybe it has to do with your speed and the placement of the thing. Taped at the edge of the blanket, the buzzer might not go off at a walk. But throwing your weight forward, when you started loping, must have supplied enough pressure to switch the thing on."

That made sense, Alec thought. He remembered that the Black started acting up only after Frank gave the signal for the riders to pick up speed.

"The real question is how it got under your saddle."

Alec's face flushed with anger. "When I find the person who put that thing there I'm going to—"

"You're not the only one, Alec."

CHAPTER 20

The Pieces Start to Fit Together

M ike was taken down to the ranch in one of the Jeeps. The rest of the crew came over to see if Alec and the Black needed any help. Wes warned them back. "Give us some space, people."

Marty stepped forward from the small crowd. "What happened to your horse back there, Ramsay?"

Alec glanced at Wes, who shook his head slightly. The movement was almost imperceptible, but Alec guessed what it meant. Wes didn't want Marty to know about the buzzer.

Alec shrugged. "He seems all right now."

Marty looked at Alec suspiciously. Wes cut in. "Don't worry about it, Marty. He's wrapped for the day. I'm sending Alec and the Black home."

"After that performance, you bet you are."

Alec traded the Black's saddle and bridle for a halter

and lead shank. As he was about to start down to the ranch, Wes pulled him aside. "Marty's no dope. He knows there's more to what happened here than the Black's temperament. We're just lucky no one got hurt."

"So where does that leave us now?"

Wes thoughtfully switched his chaw of tobacco from one cheek to the other. "Get yourself back to the ranch. And don't worry about the PSA. We'll finish the shoot even if I have to fill in for you myself."

"What about the buzzer?"

"I'll find out where that gizmo came from. You can bet on it."

Strutting to his Jeep, Wes looked back over his shoulder and half smiled at Alec. "I guess one good thing did come out of it all, though. The Black didn't have any problem with the shadows this time. That buzzer gave you both something else to think about."

Wes left Alec and hurried off to meet up with Frank. Alec wiped the sweat and grime from his forehead with the back of his hand. He reached up to stroke the Black's neck and rub his ears. "Good boy," Alec whispered. "We did it. We broke through."

Yes, Alec thought, the shadow hadn't stopped them this time. But then he frowned as he thought about the gizmo taped under the Black's saddle blanket. Like it or not, it seemed that the buzzer had put the chain of events into motion. And he didn't like it, not at all, even if it had played a part in curing the shadow problem. That thing could have gotten him or the Black—or both of them—killed. The more he thought about it, the more determined he became to find out how that buzzer found its way under his saddle.

Alec led the stallion to the other side of the box canyon. As he started down the trail, he tried to put his thoughts together. After what happened on the PSA, he could only be certain of one thing. Someone had wanted to panic the Black.

Suddenly he stopped dead in his tracks. The saddles and blankets were switched at the last minute. Maybe the buzzer in the blanket hadn't been meant for the Black at all. Maybe it was intended for Lowball and Kramer!

All along both he and Ellie had assumed that the sabotage was directed at the ranch. Neither of them had even considered that the target could be one of the actors. The idea seemed so simple, he wondered why he hadn't thought of it before.

Alec resumed his trek down the trail, anxious to talk over these new possibilities with Ellie. Finally, it seemed the pieces of the puzzle were starting to fall into place. Back at the ranch, Alec hosed down and washed the Black. Ellie came out of the office just as he finished. "You don't look so bad. Julio said the Black went loco on you."

"I feel like I've been run through the tumble cycle in a dryer."

"You should have seen Mike."

"Was he still out of it when they got here?"

She nodded. "He came to for a minute and didn't know where he was. It sounded like he thought he was still riding after you and yelling for you to hang on. Then he started saying something like, 'No, no, not again.' Jim went with him to the hospital."

Alec felt a little guilty about Mike getting hurt trying to help him. "What he did took guts. It was a little crazy, though. I mean, I know he was trying to help, but he almost drove the Black and me into the trees."

"Any idea why the Black took off like that?"

Alec told her about the buzzer that Wes had found hidden in the saddle blanket.

"Unbelievable. You say Frank made you switch saddles before the shot?"

"Yeah."

"That probably means the buzzer was meant for Lowball and Kramer!"

"I thought of that too."

"Kramer! Maybe he's the one they've been after all along!"

Alec nodded in tentative agreement.

Ellie smacked her forehead. "If I hadn't been so pig-headed in trying to pin our troubles on Sagebrush, I would have seen this a long time ago. How could I be so stupid?"

"Any idea who tacked up Lowball this morning?"

"Probably Mike. But that doesn't mean anything, if the buzzer was well hidden. It could have been anyone."

"How about Julio?"

"Maybe."

Alec scratched his head. "How many people could have guessed which saddle blanket Kramer was going to use for the PSA?"

"Anybody. Kramer's superstitious, always uses the

same gear. It kind of surprises me that he agreed to switch with you."

"You know," said Alec, "that has to be it! Kramer must be the target. Now all we have to do is start looking at people who have a grudge against him."

Ellie rolled her eyes. "That list could fill a book. And whoever the bad guy is wouldn't even have to be here. They could be paying off someone on the crew to help with the sabotage."

Ellie walked along as Alec led the Black back to the corral. She opened the gate and Alec turned the stallion loose inside. After feeding the Black a few coffee cans full of oats, they walked back to the house. Ellie said she had to get back to work. Before she disappeared into the office she told Alec to go into the kitchen and make himself a sandwich. Alec did as she suggested. Later he walked outside to sit on the porch. At Sagebrush, bulldozers churned up the dirt by the houses under construction.

Jeeps started returning from the location site. Wes came by and told Alec that they had finished the PSA with Patrick filling in for Alec. For the rest of the day the crew would be moving to the studio in town for more work on *Drover Days*. Wes walked back to his Jeep, saying he had to go to the production office for a conference.

After Wes left, Alec wandered back out to the Black's corral. He groomed his horse and stayed there awhile, just watching the Black and thinking.

For the first time since it happened, he recalled the pangs of fear he felt as the Black bore down on the line of shadow at a full gallop. What had he been scared of? And why? Were the tightening muscles he felt in the Black as they approached a line of shadow just a response to Alec's signals to hesitate, signals he didn't even realize he was sending? They must have been. All along he'd thought Wes was way off base when Wes had suggested Alec might be the one with the shadow phobia. Now he was convinced. When his life and the life of the Black had been on the line, he had forced himself not to flinch, not to worry. And the Black had responded—thank God.

When Alec stopped by to see her that evening, Ellie was at her desk in the office. She looked up from the papers she was working on.

"How's it going?" he asked.

She rubbed her eyes. "Ugh. Fine print is making me go blind."

Alec reached over and switched on the desk lamp. "Any word about Mike?"

She shook her head. The phone rang, and Ellie picked up the receiver. From what he overheard, Alec gathered someone from the hospital was on the other end. "They need an insurance card number for Mike," Ellie told Alec. "It should be in his wallet in his trailer. Want to help me look for it?"

"Sure. They say how he was doing?"

"Okay. He's resting now."

They walked out to Mike's trailer and went inside. Ellie started looking around for Mike's wallet. "You know, I was thinking some more about what happened this afternoon. Anyone could have a grudge against Kramer.

But only someone in the core crew could get close enough to do anything about it. Or one of the actors."

"Like who?"

"I don't know. Maybe one of them is jealous of Kramer or something."

"Maybe so."

Alec's gaze drifted around the room at the pictures and posters on the wall. Mike's trailer was a little Western museum all its own. Ellie picked up a pair of jeans that hung on a closet doorknob. In the back pocket she found the wallet, and inside she found the card they needed. "Here it is."

She hung up the pants again. Alec turned to leave, but Ellie didn't follow. She was staring at a dog-eared newspaper clipping tacked on the closet door.

"Hey, look at this. You know who that guy is standing next to Mike?" She pointed to the clipping Alec had noticed earlier, the one of Mike winning a trophy belt buckle at a rodeo.

"I saw that too," Alec said. "Some actor, isn't he?"

"I never noticed it before, but now that I see it close up, that looks like Kramer's old sidekick, Hank McBride."

"You mean the actor who was drowned on location, the one Jim was talking about the other night?"

She nodded and leaned closer to examine the faded clipping. "Yeah. That's McBride, all right. What's he doing with Mike?"

Reaching over to touch the paper, Alec felt the thickness at the bottom. The lower section was doubled up. Unfolding it, he read aloud the news article hidden under the photo. "Brother Gives Trophy to Brother: Harleyville—Western movie star Hank McBride, left, took time out from his busy schedule to present the awards at the Harleyville Rodeo yesterday. Top prize for bulldogging went to a familiar face on the Northwest rodeo circuit, young Mike Reynolds, who just so happens to be Hank McBride's stepbrother. Success must run in the family. Other winners were..."

Alec stopped reading and looked at Ellie.

"I knew Mike didn't like Kramer, but wow," she said. "This means..."

Alec finished her sentence for her. "Mike could still be holding Kramer responsible for what happened to his stepbrother. Didn't you know they were related?"

"He never said a word about having a brother, alive or dead. You don't really think Mike could be the one behind all this, do you?"

"I don't know what to think. Mike sure fits the profile of someone with a grudge against Kramer. And he's been there practically every time something went wrong."

"I can't believe it. He almost killed himself twice trying to stop the accidents."

Alec shrugged. "I'm not saying he did it, Ellie, just that he had a motive—revenge against Kramer. He could easily have cut the reins that caused the wagon crash. And planting the buzzer would have been a snap for him."

Ellie nodded. "You're right! He was here the day of the fire, too. In fact, he helped put it out, but not before it spread to Kramer's trailer."

Alec looked over at Mike's desk. "I think we should

look around in here a little."

Ellie started opening drawers and poking around in Mike's desk. In a wastebasket she found torn bits of black tape. She showed the tape to Alec. The tape was identical to the kind wrapped around the buzzer.

The back of Alec's neck burned with anger. "I think we better take a ride over to the hospital and have a little talk with Mike." Ellie took the clipping down from the closet door. She folded it carefully and put it in her shirt pocket.

→ **CHAPTER 21** ←

Luck

E llie phoned Wes at the production office in town
and asked him to meet her at the hospital. She
didn't tell him what they'd found in Mike's trailer,
only that it was important. Half an hour later, Alec and
Ellie were speeding down the freeway in one of the ranch
pickups.

Ellie dropped off the insurance card with a clerk on
duty in the hospital lobby. The clerk said visiting hours
were almost over but directed them to room 906.

At the nurse's station on the ninth floor they were told
that Jim had left just a short while before. No one else had
been in to see Mike. Alec turned to Ellie. "It looks like
Wes hasn't shown up yet."

"Good. That'll give us a chance to talk to Mike alone
for a minute."

They followed the numbers around a bank of elevators. The air was stuffy. The smell of antiseptic and of years of overcooked hospital food clung to the walls. The door to room 906 was open. A white-haired patient slouched on a chair inside the door. He wore a nightgown and dozed in front of a television set hanging from a mount on the ceiling. The other two roommates lay asleep.

Mike's bed was in a corner of the room beside a wide plate-glass window that had a panoramic view of the night sky. Stars glowed in misty clusters. Mike sat facing out the window, pillows propping up his back. His left leg was uncovered and wrapped in bandages.

Alec couldn't tell if Mike was dozing or lost in thought. An uneaten dinner sat on a tray table beside the bed. Ellie drew the privacy curtain separating Mike from his neighbors. Then she and Alec stepped over in front of the window. Ellie sat down on the sill. "How you doing, Mike?"

Mike didn't move but squinted as he tried to recognize his visitors. His voice sounded warm and sleepy as he spoke. "Is that you, Ellie? Alec? Hey, thanks for coming. Some spill I took, huh? The doc says I may have bruised something in my guts."

"What happened to your leg?"

"Tore some ligaments; twisted that ankle of mine again too. They got me so doped up I hardly feel it. I'll be ouchin' tomorrow, though." He tried to force a smile. Ellie and Alec didn't smile back. Out of her pocket she took the newspaper clipping. She dropped it onto his lap. Alec lay a piece of torn tape beside it.

Ellie's voice was cool. "Brought you some things from home, Mike. Look familiar?"

Mike quickly realized what they were. His expression hardened. "What were you doing in my trailer?"

"The hospital called the ranch and said they needed an insurance card for you. We were looking for it."

Mike fingered the tape and sneered. "In the wastebasket?"

Ellie came closer to Mike. "This is the same kind of tape wrapped around the buzzer Alec found in his saddle blanket." Mike turned away from Ellie. "Know anything about that?"

Up to that moment Ellie had been doing a good job of containing her wrath. Her tone of voice began to harden. "You put that thing there, didn't you? This has been about you and Kramer all along, hasn't it, Mike? Hasn't it?"

Mike hung his head. When he spoke again, his words came low and even. "All these years, I've been trying to forget. Then Kramer shows up on the set. What was I supposed to do?"

Someone came in the room and shuffled across the linoleum. Wes stepped around the curtain. Ellie ignored him. She threw up her hands and stared down at Mike. "But why, Mike, why?"

"He was my brother, that's why."

Wes looked puzzled. "Wait a minute. Brother? What's going on here?"

Ellie turned to Wes. "Mike's been keeping a little secret from us. Hank McBride was his stepbrother."

"What!"

"Mike's been after Kramer since Kramer signed on to *Drover Days*. That's why we've been having all the trouble at the ranch."

Wes stood there slack-jawed, waiting for Mike to deny Ellie's accusation. Mike said nothing. He looked like a little boy about to be punished. One of the other patients in the room started to snore.

Ellie tried to keep her voice down as she turned back to Mike. "You're not the only one who's lost someone in an accident, you know. I'm not chasing around after the drunk driver who ran into my parents."

"You were pretty young when your folks were killed, Ellie. It was different with me and Hank."

Wes stepped closer to the bed. "So you don't care about anything else? Getting back at Kramer is all that matters? Don't you realize what you've been doing to the ranch? Look at me, Mike!"

Mike stiffened, yet his voice sounded soft, almost hypnotized. "Just when I thought I'd blocked the whole thing out of my memory, Kramer shows up at the ranch. Pretty soon it all started coming back to me. If it wasn't for that creep, my brother would still be alive. It kept me awake at night, thinking. I just couldn't sit there and do nothing while...but I didn't mean to..." He started to sob.

Wes grabbed Mike by the shoulders and shook him angrily. Mike cringed with pain. "Your brother was killed in an accident, for pete's sake!" Hurt and betrayal mixed with the anger in Wes's voice. Ellie and Alec pulled Wes back.

Ellie stared down at Mike. "We were your friends, Mike. Didn't that count for anything? What about Joey? You made that horse! And why hurt Alec and the Black? What did they ever do to you?"

"Do you think I like the way things turned out? How was I supposed to guess the wagon team would head for the trees instead of just running off? Or that Frank would switch Kramer's saddle for the Black's? I didn't want to hurt anyone but Kramer."

Wes laughed in Mike's face. "Oh, I guess that's okay, then."

Alec seethed with fury. "You idiot! We could have been killed."

"I tried to stop you, Alec. That's how I ended up in the hospital." Alec shook his head in disgust.

Mike closed his eyes and leaned back in his pillows. A look of pathetic tranquility drifted across his face. Having unburdened himself of his secret, he seemed resigned to accept his fate. Come what may, it was all out of his hands.

Someone entered the room from the hall. When the nurse saw the three of them hovering over Mike, she told them visiting hours were over and that they'd better go.

Wes shook his head as he turned away. "You're all through, Mike. Don't even think about showing your face around my ranch again. I'll have your things packed up. Write us and let us know where you want them sent." Then he followed Alec and Ellie out into the hall.

They didn't say anything until they reached the parking garage. Ellie turned to Wes. "What now, Pops? Do we call the sheriff?"

Wes shook his head. "I know I should, but I'm not going to. Mike doesn't need to go to jail. That wouldn't help."

"What if he goes after Kramer again?"

"I don't think Mike will be chasing Kramer around the countryside, if that's what you're worried about. Luck brought those two together. Bad luck, but luck just the same. Don't worry. I'll keep my ears open. If Kramer so much as cuts himself shaving, the police will know where to look."

Ellie's eyes flashed with anger. "Who does he think he is, telling me I don't know what it's like to lose somebody?"

Wes looked back at the hospital entrance. "Revenge is a disease, honey, like chickenpox or measles, only you can't see it on the outside. It'll eat at a person's soul until there's nothing left but anger and hate. Mike is basically a good kid. He'll come around."

Turning on his heels, Wes walked down a row of parked cars to find his truck. Ellie scratched her head as she watched him leave. "I'll never figure Pops out. One minute he's at war with the world, the next he's Mister Let-it-be."

Alec and Ellie climbed into her pickup and drove back to the freeway. "I still can't believe this," Ellie said after a long silence. "Mike was like one of the family."

"It's like Wes said, revenge is a disease. I sure hope I never feel that way about anybody."

Soon they were pulling into the ranch driveway. It had been an exhausting day, and Alec looked forward to getting some sleep. He opened the door of the truck and stepped outside. "Guess you'll be looking for a new assistant trainer around here."

"Know anybody who might be interested?"

Alec smiled. "Not right offhand. I'll let you know if I think of someone. Good night, Ellie."

"Night, Alec." She watched him disappear into the dark.

Alec was up early on his last morning at the ranch. He rode into town to gas up the van. The ranch was quiet, except for the sounds of groaning bulldozers and construction workers coming from Sagebrush. *Drover Days* was shooting interior scenes at the studio in town that morning. Alec's plane wasn't leaving for a few hours, so he figured he had time to take one last ride up into the canyon.

When he reached the corral, he found the Black waiting for him expectantly, as if he already sensed that this would be a travel day and was eager to get going. It didn't take Alec long to feed and groom his horse. Soon they were edging their way around the barricade that marked the head of the canyon trail. The stallion moved easily, assured and totally composed. He held his head up proudly, lowering it only when stones cluttered the path at his feet. Once they arrived at the box canyon, Alec pressed the stallion into a jog. He felt the solid, pistonlike motion of the Black's legs grabbing for more dirt.

Trusting the stallion to guide them safely, Alec let the stallion have his head. He tasted the rush of wind in his face as the Black burned a path across the flat canyon bottom. It could have been seconds or minutes before he pulled up on the reins.

Alec slid down from the Black's back and fell to the ground. While the Black ripped up clumps of grass from the dry ground, Alec watched the high white clouds pass overhead. It was a beautiful morning. He lay there awhile, then rolled over and looked around.

There on the other side of the canyon lay the wreckage of the crashed wagon. He couldn't stop his thoughts from returning to that awful scene. A shudder passed through him.

Alec turned around again and sat up, trying to forget the sight of the busted-up wagon. It was no use. A horse lay buried in a fresh grave over there.

Alec called the Black to him. He knew he should be happy. Yesterday the Black had carried him through a line of shadow at top speed. They would be able to race again. Yet something nagged at Alec, keeping him from celebrating. Had he really overcome his fear of shadows? Yesterday's breakthrough had been in a life-or-death situation. How would he react under more normal circumstances? Alec had to know, once and for all. He slung himself up into the saddle and started off at a trot. Quickly the Black lengthened his strides to a thundering gallop.

Alec focused on the shadow falling from the distant stand of trees—the site of one tragedy and the haunting reminder of another. He sat very still, barely touching the Black with hands or legs. When he shifted his weight forward, the Black stretched out without hesitation, extending himself further. They drew closer and closer to the trees and the waiting shadow. Would he start sending unconscious signals to the Black, Alec wondered. If he did, the Black's reaction when they reached the shadow would tell him so.

The time had come to face his fear, Alec knew. But this time it would be in his own way and on his own terms. It would be impossible to ride the Black the way he was meant to be ridden, to truly become one with the Black, if his fear of shadows remained.

He let his mind go free, thinking of everything and nothing at the same time. Opening his mouth, Alec breathed the rushing wind deep into his lungs. "Go, Black. Go!" he cried, losing himself in the surge of powerful muscles. Wind blurred his eyes, but he wanted to keep them open, he wanted to see…everything.

Dark streaks of shadow rushed up before him. There was plenty of room to swerve if he had wanted, but instinct was guiding Alec's hands and body. He breathed regularly and kept driving straight ahead, riding without any hesitation or tension.

Even before they crossed the shadow line, Alec knew they'd be all right. Something lost had returned to Alec, something hard to describe. It was in the way he received the stallion's back, the way he spoke to his horse with legs and hands. A rush of emotion flooded him. He felt like he'd just won a race, a very private race against a very powerful rival.

Back at the ranch Alec cooled out the Black, packed his things and brought the Black in from the corral. Ellie met him at the driveway. Wes and Jim stood on the porch, watching them. Jim nudged Wes and gave Alec an exaggerated wink. Ellie and Alec walked around to the other side of the van to say good-bye to each other in private.

"This has been some trip," Alec said. "Now that it's over, I feel as if I've been playing a part in some old Western movie myself."

Ellie moved closer to Alec and smiled shyly. "Then I guess this is where you ride off into the sunset."

"Sunrise would be more like it."

"I'll miss you, Alec," she said, waiting for a good-bye kiss.

"How would a good movie cowboy handle this situation? Ah. Now I remember." He leaned over and kissed the Black on the nose, like a cowboy lonesome for the trail. Ellie laughed and shook her head. They both knew that with a little luck, things could have worked out differently between them. Maybe another time it would.

When he was done loading the Black, Alec gave Ellie a hug and a sisterly kiss on the cheek. He shook hands with Wes and Jim. The old trainer's eyes twinkled. "Come back, Alec, anytime. You and your folks should think about relocating out here. There isn't a better place for raising horses than California."

Alec grinned. "Thanks for the hospitality. If there's anything we can do..."

"I think we'll be all right now. Say hi to Henry for me."

Jim popped into the house for a second and came out again holding an eight-by-ten black-and-white photograph.

"Hey, Alec. I almost forgot to give you this. Kramer had it sent over when he heard you were leaving." He handed Alec an autographed publicity photo of Kramer in full cowboy regalia.

Alec grinned. "Henry'll love this."

A note was clipped to the photo. *Stop by my restaurant if you come back to California next year,* the note read. *I'm going to name a sandwich after you and the Black—New York style roast beef on Arabian pita bread, with carrot sticks on the side! Happy trails. Your friend, Paul Kramer.*

Alec smiled. Roast beef?

✦ ABOUT THE AUTHOR ✦

STEVEN FARLEY grew up in the two Farley homes in Pennsylvania and Florida, where there was always a horse in the backyard. After studying journalism at New York University, he worked as a circus roustabout, bookseller, set builder for commercials and rock music videos, construction worker, and long-distance truck driver from Europe to the Middle East. Now a freelance writer based in Manhattan, he travels frequently, especially to places where he can enjoy his hobbies of diving and surfing.